THE LAST BOUT

A DARK MAFIA ROMANCE - NEVER BEEN CAUGHT 4

IVY WONDER

CONTENTS

Sign Up to Receive Free Books	1
Synopsis	3
Prologue	5
1. Chapter 1	13
2. Chapter 2	19
3. Chapter 3	31
4. Chapter 4	39
5. Chapter 5	45
6. Chapter 6	55
7. Chapter 7	64
Intermission	71
8. Chapter 8	75
9. Chapter 9	85
10. Chapter 10	92
11. Chapter 11	103
12. Chapter 12	108
13. Chapter 13	117
Epilogue	122
Sign Up to Receive Free Books	125

Made in "The United States" by:

Ivy Wonder

© Copyright 2020 – Ivy Wonder

ISBN: 978-1-64808-113-2

ALL RIGHTS RESERVED. No part of this publication may be reproduced or transmitted in any form whatsoever, electronic, or mechanical, including photocopying, recording, or by any informational storage or retrieval system without express written, dated and signed permission from the author

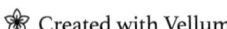 Created with Vellum

SIGN UP TO RECEIVE FREE BOOKS

Sign Up to Receive Free E-Books and Audiobook Codes.

Would you like to read **Savage Hearts** and **other romance books** for **free**?

You can sign up to receive free e-books and audiobooks by typing this link into your browser:

https://ivywondersauthor.com/ivy-wonders-author

SYNOPSIS

A champion underground boxer steps in to save a woman from her stalker, starting a hot affair between them. But when the vengeful stalker hacks his boss's computer system and starts feeding information on him to the FBI, he puts the lover, himself, and the FBI agent in the gunsights of the deadliest criminal mastermind in America.

Blurb

I haven't lost a fight in ten years.
I've ruled underground boxing in Detroit for over a decade now.
I've made a legend of myself.
But when I save an innocent girl from her stalker, I lose to her...
...in the best way possible.
I don't do serious relationships—too risky.
But Josie is different—she makes the risk worth it.
But when her stalker sets the FBI on me and my boss,
I'll have to fight like hell to protect her.

PROLOGUE

Carolyn
Date: February 16, 2019
Location: Detroit, Michigan
Subject: Jacob Todd "Jake" Ares
Criminal Record: Juvenile files sealed. Court-martialed, imprisoned for three months, and subsequently subjected to a bad conduct discharge from the US Army. His crime was repeatedly participating as a fighter in an underground boxing ring for pay at Joint Base San Antonio. Because Private Ares, then nineteen, had no other offenses, he was spared further discipline. Ares is estranged from his biological family, partly as a result of this incident.

Ares moved to Detroit in 2007, six months after his discharge, to pursue a career in professional mixed martial arts. However, he was unable to find a sponsor despite a string of victories on the amateur circuit, likely due as well to his bad conduct discharge and the reputation that it left him with.

Ares has been picked up for a few altercations in Detroit bars, but charges have been generally dropped as these have all been part of a mutual melee. He has a reputation for wading into bullying incidents to protect the victim. He has no history of violence against noncombatants.

Ares has no employment record outside of a part-time job providing security at the Iron Pit nightclub (see employment notes below). However, his lifestyle is multiple tax brackets above what his employment could possibly cover. This includes his savings from his military career.

THE WIND BLOWS hard against my hotel window, spattering the glass with heavy flakes. I look up from my computer and sigh, standing and stretching. *Damn it. I'm freezing again and can't focus.*

Outside, the snow is piling up in the crowded streets. As I walk up to the broad window and look down, a pickup truck on the street below slides into the back of an SUV to a chorus of honks. *Detroit in mid-February. Thanks so much, boss. I already miss San Diego.*

I've spent all winter running around the United States as well as both Canada and Mexico in search of suspects. They're all from a list that my boss, Assistant Director Derek Daniels, handed to me as my first long-term assignment. It includes five men suspected of serious crimes that neither the FBI nor local law enforcement has been able to successfully prosecute.

I've been closing those cases in really unexpected ways, but I've been closing them. I'm down to the last two: the really infamous one at the bottom of the list, and Jake Ares, an outlaw boxer suspected of murdering a couple of guys in the ring. Except ... nothing in his pattern of crimes or his psych profile fits with those suspicions.

I'm not buying that this guy has intentionally killed anyone.

He's a bruiser and loves a good fight. But underground fighting has a pretty high body count—and both the kills could have been accidents.

Or perhaps the ironic way that the last three of these criminal cases have ended has finally gotten to me, and I'm coming down on this guy's side irrationally. Mostly because I expect him to turn out to be just the same way: an outlaw, but not a clear and present danger to society.

I used to be such a blind idealist before I started working under AD Daniels. Innocence and goodness were determined by whether you obeyed the law or not. I didn't think twice about the character or redeemability of outlaws. And now ... Now, everything's changed.

Derek Daniels is under investigation for sexually harassing nearly every single female employee under him at the New York office, including me. He's an assistant director at the FBI with more money and power than I've ever dreamed of having. He's been doing this for years and getting away with it.

When I refused him, he stuck me with this laundry list, forcing me to run around in winter, navigating dangerous storms, canceled flights, and snow-clogged roads. And all to chase down a group of men whom he knew would be just as difficult to convict as they have been to catch.

The only reason that things are falling apart for Daniels now is that there is a gray-hat hacker out there who doesn't like how my boss treats me and has decided to intervene—the same hacker who has been helping me track these men, learn their real stories, and sort out what to do. I don't even really know why he's doing it, aside from just liking me.

The lawman hurts me and puts me in harm's way. The outlaw helps me stand up to him and fix it. The world has gone upside down ... and forced me to look at each of these men, not just as a criminal to catch, but as a human being.

I'm probably a better person for it, but I'm sure not I'm a happier person for it.

Life used to be so much simpler. And not just because I've needed to take a more nuanced look at things. I have some more basic, personal, primal needs that these cases keep reminding me aren't being met.

Going back to my desk, I bring up Ares's photos—and roll my eyes in exasperation as yet another reminder of my 'little problem' pops up on my screen. *Oh, for pity's sake—again?*

I don't know if this factored into Daniels' decision of who to put on my list, but *every single one* of these criminals has been not only morally ambiguous, but an absolute snack.

Tall, dark, and handsome guys. Blue-eyed blonds with boyish faces. The fifth case photo I can't even look at without my mouth going dry ... a smorgasbord of hunks. And I don't even date. *Is Daniels trying to torture me?* I wonder as I stare at the latest example.

Ares has the look of an athletic superstar, which maybe shouldn't surprise me. It makes perfect sense that a mixed martial artist working the underground scene looks like he was carved with lasers from a block of steel. But that doesn't help my thirst one bit as I stare at those photos.

He dresses to show that awesome body off, too—he's probably one of those guys who goes sleeveless until everyone around him is completely bundled up. Big and powerful looking, his tanned skin gleams almost as brightly as his big, rakish Hollywood smile. I don't know what kind of workout routine he follows, but it's sure paying off.

His hair is cropped so close that it's a dark fuzz. Brilliantly colored, elaborate tattoo sleeves cover both his arms. His big, almond-shaped bedroom eyes are so green, it looks like he's wearing colored contacts.

Another man so beautiful, I'd want him in my bed if I didn't know he was dangerous. But he is. Even if those deadly weapon fists of his are not wielded with the intent to kill, they had killed. I have to remain aware of that.

My job this week is to find and question him in conjunction with those two murders. If I can bring in this guy, or better yet, the leader of the illegal boxing ring, I can get out of Michigan before I freeze to death.

My exotic new laptop in the armored case pings at me, and I look over. Another email from Prometheus, my hacker guardian angel. I still know almost nothing about him aside from his reliability and extensive knowledge about the American and Canadian criminal underworld. That's what I need right now.

Daniels gives me a list, a file, a budget, and plane tickets. After that, that corrupt, half-assing burnout considers his job to be done. I've never had backup except for once, and that was when we thought we had the current Don of New York City in the bag.

Prometheus sends me gifts and information. He has kept me from walking into danger. He's kept me from taking in someone who deserved it far less than the people who had been sent after him. He's even helped me collar an infamous mob hitter who was *after* one of the guys on my list. If it wasn't for him ...

I lean my forehead against my hand as the wind rattles the insulated windowpane. *The break in San Diego wasn't long enough.*

Winter is the loneliest season: dark, cold, isolating, and full of family-oriented holidays that I've mostly had to skip this year while chasing criminals. It's affecting my mood and my judgment. Making me look forward to emails from a friendly but criminal stranger who is as likely to be using me as he is helping me.

Nevertheless, I feel a little leap of anticipation inside of me as I go back to my desk to check his message.

Carolyn,

Welcome to Detroit. I apologize for the shortness of this note, but I have business to attend to this evening. Three things that you should know as you proceed:

1. Derek Daniels is currently under surveillance due to his continuing questionable conduct and was seen completing a background check on you in search of incriminating information. Of course, he found nothing, but I doubt this will be his last quiet attempt to cause you trouble.
2. A black-hat hacker known as YokaiPrince is currently operating in this area and may intervene in your investigation of Mr. Ares. Information on his true identity and whereabouts is not yet available. When it is, you will know.
3. Mr. Ares is not a murderer. The fighting ring that employs him does not include blood sports, he had no motive, and autopsy reports of the two men will reveal the deaths to be accidental.

Have a good evening, Carolyn. I will contact you with further information when I have it.

I sit back in my seat and close my eyes, trying to focus past my disappointment that I won't be chatting with Prometheus tonight. *So, Prometheus knows about the situation surrounding Jake Ares's alleged crimes and claims that it will be impossible to prosecute. Instead, he's bringing up some local hacker that he claims is involved.*

I wonder why he brought up this hacker. Is it territoriality, or is this YokaiPrince guy really that dangerous? And how does he tie into the case?

Looks like I have a bit of research to do. That's fine. My sleep schedule is so messed up right now that I won't sleep for hours as it is. *So, let's see what you've done, YokaiPrince, and find out what it has to do with Jake Ares.*

CHAPTER 1

Jake

"Billy? Come on, man, quit playing around. I didn't even hit you that hard ... Billy?"

"He's gone, Jake. I'm sorry. It was a total accident, and we all saw that, but the boss wants to talk to you."

" ... Oh God. Wait, no, that isn't possible. He was just talking to me—"

Light. Noise. The smell of blood. Billy's blank eyes staring upward, the astonished look frozen on his face.

I sit up with a breathless little yell of shock and open my eyes to my own dim bedroom. I thrash the bedding aside and set my feet on the hardwood floor before I get control of myself, the adrenaline jolt leaving me shaking. " ... shit," I pant, staring around to get my bearings.

Billy's been dead for two years. It's just the same damn nightmare *again. Get it together.* I rub my face, then turn my head to stare at my hunched form in my mirrored closet door.

For a heartbeat, I look like two hundred and forty pounds of scared kid. Then I puff out a breath and lie back, staring up at my ceiling. *This shit never seems to get any easier.*

Two of my opponents have died in the ring. One dumb fucker, Carl, had amped himself up on something before the fight. I still don't know what, but when things got hot and heavy in the ring, he keeled over in the second round.

I was in my early twenties then, and it almost scared me out of the job. It took a private talk with the Motor City Iron Pit's owner, the big boss himself, to get me back into the ring and fighting again. Now we have blood tests like above-board leagues, and most of the time, I can fight with confidence that nobody's going to bite the dust unexpectedly.

We fight to first blood or knockout. That's it. Nobody's supposed to die.

Billy was a mistake. Not an accident—my mistake, and also Billy's. If I had known about the childhood injury that had left him with a weak neck, I never would have hit him in the face.

I didn't know. It was something he covered for by building up muscle and lying about it so he could still fight. When he went down, I swear to God I thought he was playing with me.

He wasn't.

The boss told me that it wasn't my fault. I was a veteran of too many fights to have miscalculated badly enough to kill someone. It was simply a matter of miscommunication and sheer accident.

He changed the rules again. Now he makes all fighters get a full physical every six months. He takes good care of his people; I've got no complaints there. But somehow, two years on, I still scream myself awake remembering the shocked look on Billy's dead face.

He was my best friend.

The nude woman lying warm and relaxed next to me stirs and makes a soft sound like a bird cooing before turning her face to the pillow. I'm not surprised my thrashing didn't wake her up. I spent most of the afternoon rocking her to sleep.

She's another fight groupie. I take home a few a week, make their fantasies come true, then gently let them go. All they really want from me is a good fucking and then to return to their lives somewhere in the world with no strings attached.

Everyone gets what they want. And what I want right now is relief and distraction—and maybe a chance to sleep a bit longer. It's two hours before my alarm goes off, and I want to use the time well.

Not waste it brooding on a past I can't change.

My old man's a bastard, but he did teach me a few things. *You keep moving forward*, he would tell me. Even if it hurts, you've got to take the lesson that the past teaches you, then leave the rest behind. Otherwise you'll end up carrying that weight and slowing yourself up for the rest of your days.

I have to get my mind off Billy. So, I roll over to look at the woman beside me instead.

Nude in a square of streetlight, still comfortable in the warm room, she lies on her side, generous curves catching my eyes. Her skin gleams in the semi-darkness, blonde hair tangled from sex, lipstick kissed off. I run my hands over her gently, moving down her body, and she stretches under me as I lean past her to grab another condom off my bedside shelf.

Her dark eyes open and look up at me hazily—and then widen in recognition and delight. "Hi!" I smile down at her softly. "Would you like some more?"

"Uh huh!" she manages, and I smile and bend down to bury my face between her ample breasts.

I spent an hour our first time together just exploring her

body while she cooed and trembled under my hands, so now I know how to touch her. Her fingers dig against my back as I stroke her pussy awake, waiting until she begs for it before sliding into her. She climaxes as I enter, thrashing and contracting under and around me as my finger on her clit keeps her excited.

We grind against each other like animals until Billy leaves my head, until everything leaves my head, and I shout and fuck and rocket toward climax. My frenzy sets her off again; she's screaming *yeah, yeah, yeah* in my ear loud enough to hurt, and I don't even care as I sprint toward my finish.

When I blow my load, I let out a strangled scream and screw her into the mattress hard enough that the metal bedframe creaks. I feel her contractions again as I empty myself and see her drowsy, satisfied smile a second before my eyes squeeze closed in bliss.

I'm always loud when I finish. I don't give a damn. When I collapse into her arms, she holds me, and for a while, I'm at peace.

This time, I sleep without dreams.

We shower one at a time after my alarm goes off; I toast her a bagel while I'm cooking my thirty-gram steak and blending my smoothie. I'm a whiz in the kitchen; if you're serious about nutrition, like good bodybuilders and athletes are, you learn your way around food.

We talk about nothing, then she starts talking about herself, and I start getting uncomfortable.

She's going back to Mallorca and a wealthy husband three decades older than her. She's quite happy with my pleasuring her, something her husband has never bothered with in the five years they have been married. She expresses half-joking regret that she can't bring me along—like a tanned, toned personal sex toy.

The moment she mentions the husband and starts her possessive wistfulness about making me her towel boy, my post-sex glow dissolves, and I come crashing back down to Earth. I smile. I'm polite, but firm. I have a prior commitment to the Iron Pit and its owner, plain and simple.

Half an hour later, we part company, both bundled against the cold—her to her Mercedes, me to my truck. No phone numbers are exchanged; I fully expect that a week from now, she'll remember the feel of my cock but not my address. That's how it goes with these things.

I head out early to work, not wanting to smell her lingering perfume. I'm dissatisfied suddenly, that same gnawing feeling that often haunts me after sex. I can't fully put my finger on why until I realize that I don't even know her name.

It's not enough. It's never enough. But it's a fun distraction, at least until I find someone worth keeping. Unsatisfying on some levels, but not worth getting depressed over.

The Iron Pit has turned me into a night creature; I have to tan under lamps now. My usual sleep schedule has to be weird to accommodate both daylight errands and past-midnight cage matches. It's barely eleven at night, and this is an early commute for me.

The wind's blowing hard, spawning black ice everywhere and shoving my truck sideways as it rolls down the highway. Detroit winters make me miss Texas, but I can deal with them well enough after over a decade. I set my jaw and fight my vehicle for control while watching out for other cars, which have thinned out this late hour but are still potential hazards.

Black ice kills. I see road flares and broken glass gleaming against it five times before I reach my exit and drive into the warehouse district.

I should really move over here. But even though the facility hides in plain sight, I'm not sure it's a good idea to live in the same area in case something goes down.

Maybe I'm worrying over nothing. The Iron Pit has never been raided; I've seen the police commissioner attend matches, which makes it pretty clear that the cops know about us but either don't care or are persistently directed elsewhere.

The cops are overextended. The boss runs the cleanest operation I have ever heard of, so they usually have no reason to bother us. The powers that be don't really give a shit what we do as long as nobody's dying, the press or FBI don't get wind of us, and the commish gets to see good fights.

I always turn in a good performance. I know how the business works, and I like the attention. It's the same reason I keep myself in top shape, adorn myself with the best tattoos, and show off as much of my body as the weather will allow. I'm eye candy as much as a fighter. It's costly and takes work, but it helps with women as well as with my career.

And women help with the stresses of the job, far better than booze or drugs or even the rush of the fights themselves.

But as I get older and richer, and my legend grows, that one missing piece becomes more and more obvious. I want someone to come home to. I want a woman who is there all the time, whose face I wake up to every night, and whose name I will never forget.

I'm brooding on it as I pull into the parking lot of the Iron Pit. But it's still better than brooding on Billy. My romantic life, I at least have a chance in hell of changing.

CHAPTER 2

Josie

"What do you mean, my husband called and wanted to be added to my bank account?" I can hear my heartbeat in my ears; my hand shakes as it grips my phone. "I'm single!"

"Oh dear. It's a good thing we always check." Suddenly, the cheerful bank rep on the other end sounds almost as worried as I feel. "He had your full name and address. Should I contact the authorities?"

"Yes, please do that." I don't know who Marvin thinks he is, trying to pull this, but I'm so done with him. I'd feel safer if that smelly, stalkery neckbeard is put away in jail. "I'll wait for the police to call me."

I'm lucky that Marvin doesn't know my account or social security numbers. But the information he does have is bad enough. My home address and my new phone number, which I've changed three times since he "fell in love" with me.

I'm a voice actress. I do a lot of English dubs of animes, I've done about six video game characters so far, and I fill in with audiobooks and advertising voiceovers. It's good money—but some of the fans are so horrendous that they make me want to quit.

The problem ones are always male, almost always older than me, and are that awful mix of socially clueless and misogynist that has them asking my cup size at convention panels. They tend to be rumpled, smelly, and unshaven, with little sense of personal space. And every last one of their breed seems to be both clingy and emotionally unbalanced.

Marvin is all these things and worse. He has convinced himself that we're soulmates, he ignores my restraining order on a regular basis, and he's constantly using his considerable hacking skills to try and force his way into my life. It's been six months since he first waddled up to my panel table—an encounter that I wish could be erased from history.

And I just found out that he has my home address.

He's been banned from the recording studio after showing up there twice. He's been banned from several cons, including the one I met him at, for "inappropriate conduct" toward women and girls. He probably has a criminal record and is pushing it by harassing me ... but he doesn't care.

He said to me once that I would never be rid of him until I learned to appreciate his devotion. Now, there's not a day that goes by where I don't wish he would get hit by a random bus and leave me in peace.

I'm thinking of getting a gun, because no way will I move just because he found my address in Rivertown. I'm just so tired of this: his fat, smirking face; his rotten smell; the trench coat he wears all the time—and of course, his insane behavior.

His mixture of pseudo-British formality and weeaboo Japanese. His tendency to deeply insult me in one breath, clumsily flirt in the next, attempt to "educate" me on my own industry in the third. His red-faced, angry-eyed sulkiness when denied anything. Before the stalking started, I was sick of the son of a bitch. Now I'm scared of him.

I call in the latest creative violation of my restraining order to my lawyer and the police, and then get up from my cluttered desk to walk across the heated concrete floor. My loft used to be a commercial kitchen before a fire and subsequent repairs; the old stainless-steel cabinets and counters still line the walls, giving me plenty of room for my books, comics, and models. The wet bar is just another one of those cabinets and is rarely opened unless I'm celebrating or completely stressed out.

Unfortunately, I drink so infrequently that I forgot that I ran through the last of my bottle of scotch.

"Dammit," I mutter, eyeing the small bottle of expensive sake sitting in the cabinet alone before dismissing the idea. I want to get buzzed enough to sleep, and that sixty-buck gift of imported Japanese goodness is meant for a special occasion.

Like a date with a real man, for once.

I peer outside, frowning; the lights in the building parking lot are dead again—probably from the whipping, icy wind. Winter's come late and fierce to Detroit this year; we've gotten two crazy snowstorms in the last week. The remnants sit like small, filthy icebergs on every corner and in every lot, melting slowly, only for their perimeters to turn into black ice as soon as it drops below freezing again.

It's gonna be a chilly drive to the liquor store. Think I can still pick up a bottle before it gets too cold to be out, though.

Rivertown has gone upscale in the last decade, though there are still pockets of actual warehouses here and there and the odd work-in-progress or abandoned ruin. Gentrification happens block by block with some slower to catch up than others. My block is taken up by the converted factory and its lot. As I step outside bundled in my anonymous gray peacoat, the sidewalk is comfortingly deserted.

I walk toward the parking lot entrance, fishing out the keys to my pink VW Bug as I go. *I should call my sister and let her know the latest.*

Maggie and her husband live in Arizona with three kids, far away from this crazy city that we grew up in. I envy her simple life, her stable relationship—and her comfortable lack of stalkers. I also know that she'll worry when she hears about Marvin's latest—but she made me promise to keep her up on everything.

Sometimes, I think about leaving Detroit myself. It's easy for me to take my work on the road; I just have to book time with a sound studio wherever I go and be prepared to do some commuting when video conferences won't cut it.

But this is my home. Even if I can't recognize parts of it anymore. *Do I really want to let Marvin drive me away from it?*

I'm one step into the parking lot when I see a large shape leaning against my car, arms folded expectantly. I can see the trench coat gapping around his substantial belly from here, and his trilby pulled low over his patch-bearded face. *Marvin.*

I take a step backward and yank out my phone, immediately taking a photograph of him and sending it to my police contact. Then I turn to rush back to my front door, slowed down frustratingly by the icy sidewalk. *Bastard, I hope you got frostbite lying in wait for me!*

I hear his shout behind me, his tone dramatic and furious, as if I'm tearing out his heart by running away. Then I hear the heavy thud of his boots and the jangle of his keys. I glance back to see him charging after me with a look of determination on his face, totally ignoring the slippery conditions.

Oh crap oh crap oh crap ...

I know at once that I won't be able to get up the stairs and swipe myself in before he can reach me. The last thing I want is to give him a chance to force me inside and invade my home. So instead, I have to get him someplace very public, where he won't dare pull anything, and wait there until the police come.

Fortunately, I know this neighborhood better than he possibly can after three years. I bolt across the street, dodging traffic, glad I'm in sensible boots instead of heels. There's a bar across the street and what I think is a nightclub down the alleyway right beside it.

He huffs and jangles after me; he's yelling again, still unintelligible thanks to wind and traffic noises. Tires screech and someone honks; I look back hopefully, but they haven't hit him. He's still running flat-out after me.

This guy got banned not an hour after he left my panel table for sexually assaulting a fifteen-year-old girl in an elevator. He grabbed her breast and then slapped her when she screamed at him. He had to be pinned to the floor and was bellowing and struggling until the police hauled him away.

Thinking about it now just makes me ignore the risks of falling and run faster.

Just my luck—the bar across the street is shuttered for a special event. But the glass doors of the nightclub are lit up now, showing the broad white lobby beyond, and I see a figure pass by inside.

I barely hesitate before bolting down the alley.

The jingling and the slap of Marvin's boots on the pavement are getting louder. He's panting too hard now to flap his gums— a blessing in itself. *Maybe the bastard's asthma will kick in and he'll have to stop.*

The shining glass doors of the club are like the gates of heaven in front of me. It's too early yet for the lines to form, I realize, eyes scanning the empty-looking lobby. Is there a bouncer there, a huge wall of muscle and security training for me to hide behind—or have I just trapped myself?

A stroke of luck hits: Marvin wipes out, going down with a thud and a grunt on a patch of the ice he's been ignoring. I keep going, eyes focused on the door, praying he's injured himself and won't get up again. He screams after me in that strange mix of melodrama and fury, as he tries to appeal to the heart of the woman that he thinks I am.

"You can't run from me forever! You have to let me save you from your ambitions!" It's even more out of nowhere than usual. He's babbled at me before that women shouldn't have ambitions —that our purpose and only happiness is to play a support role to a man. Preferably him.

This time, though, the same words are coming out of his mouth while he's chasing me down with all the crazed fury of an axe murderer. A glance back shows that he's on his feet again, beet red, hat lost behind him, gaining on me. Then I'm at the door, pounding on the armored glass in desperation, staring into the empty lobby beyond for any sign of the figure from before.

Come on, come on! I don't know if the behemoth lumbering up behind me has a gun or just plans to rape me to death, but he's starting up a throaty chuckle as he catches up. It fills me with fury and terror as I look up at the security camera pleadingly.

"Somebody let me in!" I cry out in desperation. I wish I armed myself before leaving home. *I wish I never left to get the fucking scotch.*

The door lock clicks open with a buzz and I yank the door open, then slip through and close it behind me—practically in Marvin's face. I hear him slam into the glass and then start pounding on it as I bolt through the empty, anonymous-looking reception area.

"Thank you, security guy! I'll bake cookies for you. Kiss my ass, Marvin—" I gasp under my breath as I run for my life.

Whoever let me in isn't showing himself. I race past a bank of elevators across from a set of unmarked doors, and through that into what looks like a ticket lobby. *The actual nightclub must be upstairs. I guess they don't open until midnight.*

I can hear Marvin's muffled screaming as he keeps trying to break through the glass. I have no idea what he's saying, but I can make an educated guess.

Wait, milady! Fate has brought us together!

You frigid fucking whore, you should be grateful that I give you this much attention!

If you didn't want this, you shouldn't have advertised yourself by working in anime!

He only really has about two dozen phrases that he uses, switching them up but otherwise barely deviating. It's like he's working from an English phrasebook written by someone who has never spoken to a woman in his life. It would be comedic if he wasn't so menacing.

Then he stops banging and yelling and goes quiet. I look back, making sure he hasn't somehow gotten in, only to see him hunkered down at the glass, rummaging at something in his bag. *What's he doing?*

It doesn't matter. Just keep going! He's not giving up, so I'm not slowing down. I run out into the lobby on the far side of the building, where the back parking lot lets patrons in.

A black pickup pulls into one of the parking spaces up front, and I head that direction, praying that whoever it is is friendly and can help.

Then I hear an awful sound: a sound of betrayal or maybe just a mistake. The buzz of the door behind me again. The security guy is letting Marvin in.

"Oh, no, no, no. What are you doing—!" I scramble for the

back door as he explodes through the front and comes pounding toward me across the marble tile. I reach the doors—and to my horror, discover that they have security card locks for both sides.

Marvin's already passing the elevators. I'm trapped.

Desperate, I start banging on the door and shaking it, trying to get the attention of whoever's driving that truck. "Come on! Don't leave me in here and just watch—"

A meaty hand grabs me by the ponytail and yanks me backward—then slams me face first into the glass. Marvin doesn't have much strength after all that running, but he makes up for it in vicious enthusiasm.

"Bitch!" he splutters as my face hits home.

I struggle to keep my feet under me as he drags me back again—and then slams me again into the glass. This time I just barely turn my head enough to save my nose, which is already bleeding.

"You want to knock on the door, bitch? You want to knock on the door? Here! Let's knock!" *Bam.* "Let's knock again!" *Bam.*

Pain rocks down my neck with each blow; his stench fills my nostrils as he pants and curses his way through trying to bash my face in. I see a smear of blood on the glass and wonder if the asshole in the truck has just stopped to watch. *I'm going to die from this,* I think, my ears ringing so hard that for a moment I think the buzzing noise is just part of it.

I realize that it was the buzzer to the door next to me when I feel the cold air and hear Marvin's yell of horror cut off with the sound of a blow. His grip on me shifts; he lets out a panicked whimper and yanks me around to shove me between himself and someone else like a shield.

"You can't hit me now or you'll hit her!" he wheezes as that someone looms over us both.

"Let her go," a deep, male voice growls, his Texas drawl thick in every word. "Right now. Or I will knock your teeth down your throat."

"This is between me and my wife!" Marvin whines, cowering behind me.

The ringing in my head is fading. I blink pain-tears from my eyes and look up into the handsome, stony face of a man a head taller than Marvin.

"I'm not his wife," I gasp out. "He's my stalker."

Marvin starts huffing between his teeth. "How can you say that, my love?" he cries, voice cracking in panic.

"He chased me here and someone let him in. Please don't listen to him!" I look up into the man's brilliant green eyes ... and see them narrow as his gaze shifts from me to Marvin.

"You have three seconds," he instructs the panting creep at my back. "Let go of her and step back. Three ..."

"No, no, you misunderstand!" Marvin cries out, clutching me closer. Gagging, I drive my elbow back into his gut; it thumps ineffectively into the layers of down and fat, and he yanks hard on my hair. "Behave!"

"Two ..." The newcomer's voice is getting colder with every word.

Marvin's voice rises to a panicked screech. "You can't just step in and—"

"One." The man in front of me turns into a dark blur for a split second, and I hear a noise like someone smacking a side of beef. It happens literally right above my head, so close that I feel the breeze from the man's fist.

Marvin loses his grip, and I stumble forward against the man's chest. It's like walking into a tree trunk. He slings an arm around me briefly to steady me, then lets go and moves past me as Marvin stumbles back.

I turn, leaning hard against the doors as I try to sort what just happened. *I just got rescued. But who is this guy?* He must have been driving the truck and ran in to help after all.

Marvin is bleeding a lot more than me. Blood squirts from between his fingers as he clasps both hands to his face and wails in a muffled, nasal voice. "Oh my God. Oooh, what did you do? Why did you do that?"

The man standing over him out-masses him and all the extra seems to be pure muscle. He's in a leather jacket and well-worn jeans, his dark hair cropped close—which makes his gorgeous eyes stand out even more. He looks like the kind of man who has women falling all over him all day long. A movie star. A sports star.

He also looks like he's containing more fury than Marvin ever dreamed of spewing out. "Warned you. Multiple times. Gave you a damn countdown, too. Not my fault you didn't listen, you whiny bitch."

Marvin starts spitting out lawsuit noises. The man chuckles and folds his powerful arms across his chest, his leather jacket creaking slightly as it strains over his muscles. "Security cameras caught you chasing down and beating this woman, and I guarantee she'll testify against you, not me."

"You uh ... absolutely sure you wanna bring lawyers and cops into this? Because you'll lose." He glances at me, concern flickering into his expression, before turning a smirk back on Marvin.

I run my fingertips over my face. My nose stings and is bloody, and one of my cheekbones feels badly bruised. Otherwise, I'm fine—and a lot better than I would be if this guy hadn't come along.

Marvin isn't listening. He keeps yelling "I'm gonna *sue!*" and "What's your *name?!*" and "She's *mine*. Keep away from her!" in the same gulping, explosive tone as a baby crying.

The man sighs and pulls out his cell phone, dialing up someone. "Yeah, this is Jake. Some asshole chased a woman—eh? Oh, you caught that? Why didn't you send some guys down?"

He listens for a few seconds. "Okay, well, send a couple of guys to hold him, and I'll look after the girl." Another pause. He nods. "Yeah, you got it." He hangs up and shoves the phone back in his pocket. "Okay, we're hanging out until the security guys get here."

Marvin draws his hands down from his bloody face and stares at them in horror. Then his face crumples and darkens again—and he lunges at me.

I duck out of the way just in time, and he smacks into the armored glass door. I stumble back from him, stomach clenching in panic, as he turns and bares his stained teeth at me. "This is all your fault! You provoked me!"

He rushes me again—and stops short as Jake scruffs him by the collar of his trench coat and shoves him back against the wall.

"Siddown!" the bruiser yells at him—and Marvin slides to the ground, staring up at him, white-faced. "That's better. Now stay there."

My rescuer turns and his brilliant green eyes fix on me, suddenly full of worry. "You okay, little lady?"

"Don't listen to him, Josephine! He's a filthy Chad! You belong with me!" Marvin freezes as Jake turns a deathly look on him.

I nod, hand to my face. Nothing broken. I'm not raped, stabbed, shot, or beaten to death. Someone came to help after all ...

... someone extraordinary.

"I could probably use an ice pack," I admit hesitantly, and he nods.

"Don't you worry about that, we've got 'em downstairs. Let's just get this jackass squared away once the security guys show up, and I'll help you get cleaned up." He flashes me a dazzling smile, which I return painfully.

Marvin starts sobbing like a snotty kid caught stealing, and my terror starts to melt away. I'm saved.

CHAPTER 3

Jake

IF THERE'S one thing that I hate, it's bullies. Especially when they target women.

The three times that I got in trouble at school, it was for fighting—but not for bullying. The difference seemed to fly over my parents' heads, just as it had for the school administration, but it still exists. I'm more than justified in diving in on some bastard who has decided to pick on someone smaller and less savage than him.

When I saw that slovenly creep tossing around a sweet-faced, delicate-looking girl like that, I lost it for a few moments. I barely remember rushing across the pavement, swiping my card, and kicking the door open. Time didn't turn normal again until the moment my fist smashed into his reddened, smirking face.

I could have hit him a lot harder. I wanted to. But all I could think of was getting him away from her. There was no point in hospitalizing him when making him bleed was enough, even if he was a filthy waste of skin.

Once the security guys in their unmarked black uniforms have showed up to bundle off the rumpled, furious stalker, I turn to the woman I saved from him and look her over.

She's young, small, and fragile-looking, a bruise already blooming on her pale cheekbone. Silky-looking dark brown hair falls to her shoulders, tangled by the wind; her soft gray eyes are enormous and shy, their gaze flirting with mine before flicking away again. She's bundled up, but I still catch hints of her slim curves beneath the peacoat.

Her tiny smile is like a sunbeam breaking through storm clouds.

I tear my eyes away from the delicate curves of her lips and raise them to meet her gaze. "Is there someone you can call?" I ask gently; she seems to still be in shock.

"He broke his restraining order and attacked me," she mumbles, holding her face, her eyes avoiding mine. "I should call it in to the cops. Too, um, late to call anyone else."

Cops? Shit. Of course, she has no idea what this place is, or why we don't want the police involved. "We have him on surveillance with live witnesses. The security head will want to talk to you about it. Your case is in the bag at this point. Don't overextend yourself."

She blinks up at me, and a look of relief washes over her face. "Is it really over?"

"You mean the part where that guy gets to chase you around and beat on you? That's over. If you want, I'll keep an eye on you myself until you feel safe enough to go home."

That means keeping her with me through the match, but ... I already know I won't mind that one bit. If the violence doesn't freak her out, anyway.

"O-okay." She's fishes a baby wipe from her shoulder bag and mops off the drying blood. She only winces a little; clearly, she's tougher than she looks, but she's very rattled.

"What's your name?" I look her over a bit more as she's pulling herself back together. There's a cluster of anime-themed buttons on her white leather bag, which has charms of chibi monsters hanging from it.

"Josie. I um ... thank you for saving me. I didn't actually say that, did I? I should. Thank you." She's flustered, chattery.

Better than frozen in terror, but not by much. I want to go downstairs to the holding cell and hit that guy again.

"Hey, look, no problem. I hate guys like that." I smile at her, offering a hand. She hesitates, and takes it, her slim, gloved fingers tracing across my palm timidly and vanishing in my careful grip. "I'm Jake. Let's get you that ice pack."

On the brief elevator ride downstairs, she stands still, eyes closed, as if she's still convincing herself that her rescue wasn't a dream. I'm not sure what I can say that would help, so I leave her to it. At least she's not hysterical.

Each of the star fighters has a suite in the first sub-basement. With my ten-year win record, mine's the biggest. I lead her through the steel door into the warren of concrete rooms beyond, which I've tried to make less tomblike with mirrors, plants, and natural-spectrum lights. At least it's never cold or damp down here. "Have a seat. You want music?" I pause beside the stereo on the way to my gym room.

"Jazz if you have it," she murmurs, frowning at her reflection in one of my posing mirrors.

"I do." I'm more of a hard rock guy, but jazz is easier when I have a headache, and she probably has a killer one. I put on an Ella Fitzgerald collection and go to fetch her ice pack.

"So, what do you do?" I ask as I rummage through my minifridge's tiny freezer shelf for an ice pack of the right size. It's pretty clear from the way she's looking around at all my fighting gear and memorabilia that she's just starting to understand what *I* do. She'll probably also quickly realize why this place has so much security.

Then again, we saved her ass. I doubt she'll have a problem keeping secrets, especially if the boss compensates her. Which he probably will once he learns all the messed-up details. He's that kind of guy.

"I'm a voice actress. Animation mostly." She smiles—and then winces as the expression aggravates her bruise. "Ow." She hastily takes the ice pack I hold out to her and puts it over the injury.

"That's cool. You've probably figured it out by now, but I'm a fighter. The arena's actually downstairs."

"You're ... a boxer?" She lifts an eyebrow only slightly.

"Mixed martial artist." Her surprised expression amuses me; I grin briefly. "Bet you didn't know what this place is."

"I had no idea. I honestly thought it was a nightclub." She touches her lower lip with one finger. "Nice clothes, fancy cars, crowds after midnight."

"Oh, it is. There's one upstairs that the boss also owns. Perfectly above board. But I work downstairs."

She continues examining the room, taking in my rack of practice padding, the vintage boxer posters framed on the walls, the row of kettlebells I couldn't fit into my workout room. "Downstairs is a private sports arena?"

"Very private." She hasn't quite gotten it yet, but that's fine. I don't actually want to give her too many details. "Part of the reason that the security manager will probably want to talk to you."

"Is ... he the one who buzzed me in? Because someone let Marvin in, too, or I could have just hidden in here." She looks so worried that I know she's not exaggerating, and probably not mistaken.

What the hell, Dave? "Okay, that's just messed up. Hang on a second." I pull out my phone while she nods and keeps icing her face. Calling the security manager back takes half a second. "Yo, Dave, we've got a problem."

"What?" I can hear a couple of security guys chattering in the background. "Shut up!" he snaps at them and they go quiet. "What were you saying, Jake?"

"Somebody let the guy in who was chasing her. Just buzzed him in after her. Was that your call? Because she's sort of upset." I say it in a tone that makes it clear that I'm *sort of upset* myself over this.

"He didn't have a card? The system registers a swipe-in." I hear a rustle and a click of computer keys. "Yeah, it says he got in using a janitorial ID card."

"Well, obviously he doesn't work here, so what's going on? Did he steal it?" I turn to Josie. "They didn't let him in. They say the system says he had a card."

She goes very pale and her eyes widen. "Oh God. I had no idea Marvin could work that fast." She stares me in the eyes earnestly. "Look, they need to search him for anything *computery*. The guy's a hacker. He stole a lot of my information—that's how he tracked me down."

"Shit. Okay." I get back on the phone. "You hear all of that?"

"Yeah, I heard it." He sounds resentful. "Why'd she take this long to warn us?"

"Fuck off, Dave. She's barely stopped bleeding," I growl, even more annoyed. I don't know if he's drunk on the job again or if he's broken up with another girlfriend—or both—but he's off his game and needs to stop blaming others. "Why haven't you searched him already?"

"That doughboy? How could he be dangerous? You already

made him cry." A far-off buzz gets some exclamations and chatter. "We checked him for weapons."

I roll my eyes. "The guy's a hacker, Dave. Did you check him for *electronics*?"

Just then, the lights flicker, and I hear a faint alarm go off. Dave swears under his breath and I wince, closing my eyes. "I'm taking that as a no."

Chaos erupts on the other end of the line, and I facepalm, making a mental note to call the boss about this. "Call me back when you have this in hand. Take this seriously for once—he was trying to kill her, not deliver a damn valentine."

I hang up and turn to my guest, who is sitting there very still, her face pale. "Oh God," she mumbles.

I see the dam about to break and that bullied look of panic, and my stomach drops.

"Oh, hey, wait. No, no, no. Come on. Don't cry. Don't let this fucker make you cry again." I crouch in front of her, catching her gaze, and she barely manages a wobbly smile. "Okay. Okay, that's better.

"Just hold on. That guy isn't getting through me, honey, even if he gets through that door." I hold her gaze ... those big, lovely eyes that would make me want to stare even if I wasn't trying to get her attention. "Understand?"

She swallows and nods, tears brimming in her eyes still but her despair draining away.

I give her the most reassuring smile I can muster. "Good. I've never lost a fight, little lady, and I'm not losing the one for you."

I realize how that sounds even as it's coming out of my mouth and see a flicker of something in her expression that I don't recognize. Then she blushes and glances away. "Um. Thank you, Jake."

"Why don't you tell me what this bastard has been up to? I think I'm gonna have to tell the owner. Dave has obviously fucked up, and I don't want you paying for it, so it's time to go over his head." I stay where I am, heel-sitting close to her.

This close, I can smell a delicate, slightly spicy floral perfume rising from her skin and hair. It's nice. So is watching her relax in my presence. I wonder how long it's been since she's felt safe.

"There are a lot of anime fans who are just wonderful. But then there's this minority who get ... overinvested. This guy Marvin showed up at a convention I did a signing at six months ago, and he's been stalking me ever since." Her lips tremble.

I bring her a bottle of water and she sips at it, nodding thanks before continuing. "He never really told me why he picked me. I guess I did the English dub for one of the characters he obsesses over, and that touched him off. Which is even more weird and creepy, since I've been doing this since I was fifteen and some of my characters are as young as nine."

I lean back, the corner of my eye twitching. "Ew."

"Yeah, and I'm petite and look young for my age, even when I dress like I'm about forty. It's the big eyes." She sets the bottle down and puts the ice pack back on her cheek. "He decided that I'm his dream girl and that I don't get to say no."

"I shoulda hit him in the nuts instead," I grouse a bit loudly, and she lets out a nervous little laugh. "Sorry," I mutter, ears prickling. "But seriously, what the hell?"

She actually laughs a little; I smile with relief and drag over a chair to sit in.

"I've had to deal with socially awkward fans before and even some real assholes," she tells me. "Dick pics, the usual garbage that women online get when we get even a tiny bit famous." She sobers. "But this is different. There's so much hatred right below the surface with Marvin. If I don't act like his perfect doll and play to his fantasies exactly, it's like I have to be punished."

She goes on from there, telling me about the stalking, the

restraining order, its violations, and him finally showing up tonight at her home, which is across the street from our back entrance. The privacy invasions, his creepy emails, even doxxing her was nothing compared to that.

Finally, she finishes, tears in her eyes again as I stare at her incredulously. "All that bullshit in six months?" I breathe, and she nods.

My phone rings and she jumps slightly. I answer. Dave.

"Well, he got through the cell door's electronic lock and rabbited on us," he says way too casually. "If he's still in the building, we'll catch him soon. Otherwise he's in the wind."

Fuck you, Dave. "Well, ain't that fine and dandy. You had better tell the boss." He starts to stammer and then mumbles that he'll take care of it and hangs up quickly.

I stare down at my phone. "Goddamnit. Good job fucking things up, Dave."

Then I hear Josie's soft whimper of distress and turn to see that those threatening tears are finally falling. *Aw man.*

I'm going to personally kick this guy's ass when I find him. "Josie?"

"I can't go home," she whispers. "He knows where I live."

That's when I make a decision that maybe I'll regret, but right now it not only feels right, it feels like the only thing to do that doesn't make me a callous asshole. "Then tonight you're not going home. I'm putting you up someplace safe, and I'm not leaving you unguarded until the police grab the prick. Okay?"

Her eyes widen in shock. "You'd do that?"

I nod grimly. "I told you. I hate bullies. This guy has to be stopped. The police are three steps behind and now Dave's fucked up. "I won't," I tell her firmly. "You can count on me."

CHAPTER 4

Josie

NOBODY'S EVER PROTECTED me from anything before.

As I look into Jake's brilliant green eyes, the idea of him lending all his strength to keep Marvin from getting to me washes over me and has a strange effect. I go warm all over and feel the terror start to dissolve. Maybe I should question why this total stranger would do so much for me, but ... I can't change what it's doing to my emotions.

Or my body.

"So, here's the deal," he tells me. "I've got a match tonight. I'll get you a seat to watch if you like and someone to sit with you. One of my buddies watches all the matches. I'm sure she'll do it. Nobody ever messes with Cynthia."

I've never watched a mixed martial arts match before, let alone an underground one. And no way am I walking out of this building unaccompanied. Marvin isn't going to let this go, and I can't trust the cold to drive him indoors. "I ... I think I'd like that. But what about after?"

He smiles slowly, and I see a faint gleam in his eye that makes me feel more dizzy and flustered.

"The boss owns a hotel by the airport; he puts up his VIP guests there and shuttles them in via limo for the matches. I'll snag you a room for a few nights."

I watch as he dials in and makes the reservation, just like that. This guy seems to have all the answers. It's so easy to put my trust in him that I feel myself sliding deeper into infatuation the more that he takes charge.

"Okay," I murmur breathlessly. *He may just be being nice,* I try to remind myself. *Or, he may just want to sleep with me.*

The problem is, either one would disappoint me in different ways. If he's not being nice, I won't want to sleep with him. But if he's *just* being nice, I don't have a chance with him. *Am I just being fickle?*

I've never thought I *would* have a chance with a magnificent hunk of man like this. He's everything Marvin isn't—including gentle enough that all that massive strength and imposing size just makes me feel safer. Sitting there looking up at him, I wonder what it would be like to be in his arms.

Focus. It would be great to get Marvin out of my head for the night and think about this guy instead, but I still have to focus.

"Okay," I force out. "But what about the police?"

"Until Dave gets his shit together and sorts out where the guy went, we have a problem. We can't have cops in here." His voice is firm, and I'm not too surprised; what they're doing in this place isn't legal, after all.

Heart in my throat, I nod ... and perversely feel the heat deep in my belly only intensify. I've never been part of anything illegal in my life, especially knowingly.

"What about telling them that someone saw him lurking around my car? Then they can look for him in the neighborhood without bothering me—or you."

He considers, then nods. "That's smart. I'd wait until after the match, though. If he's lying in wait for you in your parking lot or outside your building, you may as well let the fucker freeze for a while. It's not like he'll run off all the way. Like you said, he's obsessed."

I set a reminder for myself with an alarm in three hours, so I don't wear out so much that I forget. "I'm still worried about what he might do with his computer skills. He really is quite good."

"Yeah, well, I'd turn off the GPS on your phone and avoid any check-in functions like on Facebook. That way he can't track your location."

I still have my phone out and do so at once. "I didn't even think of that. Thank you." *Crap! Is that how Marvin figured out where I was?*

"Yeah, well ..." His smile goes lopsided. "I'm willing to bet you don't have to deal with too many scumbags. But unfortunately, I've had to a lot."

"You don't seem like the type," I venture, and he laughs.

"Oh, honey, plenty of folks on the wrong side of the law are still on the right side of everything else. Only reason I'm fighting here instead of the UFC circuit was that I couldn't get a legit sponsor. Here, I can't get titles and awards, but I can get a great big pile of money, and the boss treats us right."

"But you still have to deal with scumbags." I keep drinking water; the storm of tears and adrenaline has left me worn out and thirsty.

"Oh yeah. Dave's no prize—he's fucked things up twice now. The first time was when he let a random group of drunk college students downstairs instead of up to the nightclub because they paid him a pile of cash. Greed and Jack Daniels judgment.

"Some of the other sponsors or spectators are corrupt politicians, drug lords, people like that. Or they hire someone crappy or bring someone like that along in their entourage. Working in the underworld, dealing with terrible people is an occupational hazard."

I bite my lip gently as I look up at him. "Is Dave going to be a problem for me?" More than he already is, anyway; his negligence has endangered me at least once so far. If he hadn't let me into the building in the first place, I would be a lot more pissed off.

Jake laughs. "Oh no. Not with me around, baby. Dave knows better than to challenge me when I make a promise to a lady."

He winks, and my heart leaps, my stomach gets fluttery, and I forget how to breathe for a few heartbeats. *He's got me wrapped around his finger,* I realize, and offer a wobbly smile. "I'm glad, Jake. Nobody's ... done anything like this for me before."

"Sounds like you never had a boyfriend do his damn job, then." He sounds disgusted with those hypothetical boys ... but I jump to correct him.

"More like I've never had a boyfriend."

Everything stops inside me. *Oh crap, why did I just say that?*

It catches his attention before I can move on or call it a joke; he stares at me, eyes widening slightly. "You're kidding me. You're fucking adorable. Did you grow up in a colony of blind people?"

I *giggle*. It comes out of me like bubbles out of soda, all in a rush, while my cheeks get hot, and I can't look at him anymore. *Shit. What is happening to me?*

Too much time on the emotional rollercoaster. The lows I've been stuck in almost constantly for six months. The highs are unfamiliar, leaving me disoriented and breathless.

"No, I just ... never had time." I take a deep breath, closing my eyes, remembering. "My parents were Broadway stars. My mom did that stage-mom thing and dragged my sister and me into the life, and so I had both a job and school since I was ten."

"You uh ... wait. You were on the stage locally? How come I haven't seen you in anything?" He tilts his head, the light catching in his green eyes.

I open my mouth to ask why a guy like him knows the local theater circuit, then realize I'm stereotyping him and just explain.

"Because my sister and I emancipated ourselves when I was fifteen, and I switched over to voice work only. I needed my privacy during high school, and afterward, I liked it better." I don't even like thinking about my early days in the business. But at least I came out the other side and moved on to a good life.

Until Marvin came along. But maybe now I have a way out. Marvin may have just pissed off a group of people who he can't stand up to.

Jake frowns, processing the information about my crazy teens, and then his lopsided smile returns. "Well, I sure can see why you didn't have time to date with a crazy schedule like that. Teenage dating is a mess, though. You didn't miss much."

That makes me snort. "Yeah, my friends tell me stories. It doesn't sound very fun at all." I'm kind of glad he went past asking about the whole mess with my family.

I don't want to bring my mood down again by elaborating on the details of how my mother fucked up my childhood while my father stood by. It's all very straightforward: growing up too fast, having my parents squander my money while pushing me to make more, then taking charge the only way I knew how. I've already left those years in the dust, like I hope to leave Marvin.

"Yeah, I tried that scene. Thing is, I was on the football team, so everybody expected me to hit up the cheerleaders. You never met a pettier, crueler group of girls. Holy shit." He gets a text on his phone and checks it. "Okay, so my friend will be down in a bit to escort you to the arena. I have to start warming up soon or I'd do it myself." He gives me an apologetic shrug.

"It's not a problem." It is a problem. I want to cling to him like to a ship's mast in a squall. But I know that's both stupid and an overreaction.

Still, I couldn't have asked for a better group of people to hide behind.

CHAPTER 5

Josie

AS IT TURNS OUT, Cynthia is a statuesque, athletic blonde who grins hello when she sees Jake. My thoughts immediately go the route of a crushing teenager: *is this the girlfriend? The wife? I didn't see a ring but that doesn't really mean anything...*
Stop it, Josie. You barely know the guy and you're getting possessive?

"Hi." I force a smile, holding out a hand.

She clasps it firmly, pumps once and lets it go. "Hey, kid. Heard you were having a shitty day. What does this asshole after you look like again?"

"Six foot, maybe three hundred pounds, messy red hair and beard, trench coat, trilby hat, pale, dramatic." I can't remember his eye color suddenly. The color of his teeth is more memorable.

She sees my expression and sets her jaw, nodding. "Nobody like that is getting near you, honey. I'm on the job until my bro here wins, gets his shower, and can get back to you."

My smile gets a little less forced. "Thank you."

I don't want to leave Jake's side right now, but he's got work to do—crazy, dangerous work that I never thought I would see with my own two eyes. He smiles calmly and confidently as he waves us off; it's an adventure to me, but to him, it's Tuesday night.

"Take good care of her, Cyn. I'm counting on you."

"Don't worry. I'll get her back to you in one piece." She looks down at me as she leads me off. "You look pretty worn out. You need a sports drink or something?"

"Maybe. The water helped." I look back once, but Jake has already closed his door, probably to change. "Are you one of the fighters?"

"Yeah, the boss doesn't do sexism. Especially since I can get butts in seats nearly as well as Jake." She chuckles when she sees my purse charms. "You really do voices for video games and such?"

"Some. Most of my work is anime dubs. But unfortunately …" I trail off, thinking about Marvin and hoping he isn't smashing in my door as we speak.

"You ever think of taking some self-defense courses?" She leads me to one of the elevators as we talk. She hits the button.

"I was thinking of buying a gun and getting in some range time," I admit, and she gives me an amused look.

"Going straight to that? I can't really blame you. But Jake and I could teach you some shit that will let you win out over a bullying creep like that without a gun. If you're interested, of course." She looks me up and down.

"He's like three times my mass," I point out, and she just laughs.

"Bruce Lee weighed 140 pounds and could kick even Jake's ass, honey. It's not about how big you are. It's about how hard you train." The elevator arrives and opens, and we step inside. "Honestly because most of his mass isn't muscle, he's at a serious disadvantage against people who know what they're doing."

This is so far out of my league that all I can do is nod and listen. She leans against the far wall, folding her arms, and looks at me seriously. "First things first, though. This guy knows where you live, and he's really good with computers and electronics."

"That's right. He got through your outside security door somehow. I don't know enough about computers to figure out how, but this place seems pretty high tech, so ... that should give you some idea of why I'm worried." I glance up at the security camera, hoping that Marvin isn't somehow staring at me through it right now.

"Fucking Dave. You know, we've tried with him, but when Katie hired him, I had a bad feeling, and it's played out just as I thought it would." Her scowl reminds me of Jake's. "At least he buzzed you in when that guy was running up on you."

"Yeah." I close my eyes and lean back against the elevator wall. "He did. And then Jake showed up and did the rest."

"You were lucky. You let us teach you some stuff, and you won't have to rely on luck." Her voice is a little harder than Jake's, but there's warmth in it, too. She seems to mean well.

I open my eyes and look up at her, and nod. "Okay. I mean, you guys have done so much for me already, but ... that's something I want. I don't want to be scared anymore."

She grins widely and thumps me gently on the shoulder. "There ya go. We can talk about scheduling you after the match. Now let's stop by my dressing room and get your makeup fixed."

I'm shocked when we get there, and this Valkyrie of a woman sits me down in her makeup chair and starts fussing over me like a backstage matron. "You clean up pretty well," she comments as she works.

"Thanks. I used to be on stage as a kid. I quit to do the voice work." I hesitate, but ... *no time like the present.* "So how did you and Jake meet?"

"We train together along with the other fighters. The boss sponsors ten of us—four women and six men. We fight each other. We fight guests. I met him six years back in the weight room." She laughs a little. "His accent was so thick back then that people used to ask what cattle ranch he grew up on. Then he kicked everybody's ass in the ring at least once, and they stopped laughing and started buying his beers."

"Wow." I smile a little—and then stop talking as she starts brushing on my lipstick.

"Yeah. Anyway, we hit it off pretty fast, learned a lot from each other, and he actually gets along with my family, so ... pretty much my bestie." She tilts her head slightly and meets my gaze in the mirror. "You're not crushing on him already, are you?"

I watch my face in the mirror turn red. "U-um ..."

She snorts and starts adding the sealer. "That's a big yes."

Oh crap. Guess I don't know how to hide my feelings well even now. "Well, he did save me, and he is ... um ..."

"Hot," she finishes, and I let out an awkward squeak that makes her snicker. "It's okay. If I wasn't married to Henry, I probably would have hit on him pretty hard myself. And if you want to play, well ... he'll treat you right."

Is it possible to die of embarrassment? "I don't know anything about ... playing," I mumble in the direction of my shoes.

"Oh really? Well, don't let him know that, or you'll have him volunteering to help. He gets a kick out of being a lady's first time." Her eyebrows jump briefly. "Or you could just catch him after a fight or a big workout."

Oh my God. I already pretty much told him I'm a virgin. But then what she just said catches in my head, and I manage to look up at her. "Sorry? Won't he be tired and hurt?"

"Hurt? Not too badly. The guy's a rock. Tired? Oh, honey. Between the adrenaline and the hormone release from a good workout, he's gonna be up for hours. If you know what I mean." Her eyes twinkle.

"Um ...?" I don't. And then I do. And my eyes widen, and I'm quiet for a while as she fights laughter. *Oh. Oh my.*

He's taking me to a hotel room after this while he's feeling ... like that. And all I have to do is ... offer. I swallow hard, my whole body humming with excitement and desire.

It's so tempting. Not just because the chance is there, not just because he likes me and I want him, not just because it's the perfect ironic revenge on Marvin after everything he's done. But because I want the chance to rest in Jake's arms and sleep safe and sound, like I haven't been able to in months.

"I'll keep that in mind," I squeak, and she laughs as we get ready to leave her dressing room and find our seats in the arena.

This place is so thoroughly soundproofed that I'm actually shocked when we get back into the elevator and find it crowded. The people stuffed inside are so diverse that they look like they're going to different events. Punk rock types and athletes rub elbows with rich people in fancy suits and glittering gowns.

Cynthia ignores them all as she chatters at me about the fights, their rules, their standards, and what Jake will be facing tonight. "Some guy from Thailand. They churn out some seriously badass fighters, but I don't know much about this one. His sponsor worked out a deal with the boss for him to be a guest."

"How ... dangerous is this?" I ask tentatively as the elevator rumbles downward. "Jake's never actually been badly hurt fighting like this, has he?" He's strong, he's my hero, but I don't want him to bleed.

"Jake hasn't lost a fight in ten years," Cynthia replies simply, her voice gaining even more confidence. "If he's gonna lose anytime soon, it won't be tonight."

I remember how he moved when he was rescuing me. My eyes couldn't even track it. I know he held off on really hitting Marvin hard, but all it took was that one single, precise blow to turn my obsessed, stubborn, evil fuck of an attacker into a blubbering pile of uselessness.

"I believe you. I've never seen anyone stop a fight so fast." The moment that Jake made Marvin let go of me still feels a little like a miracle.

The elevator spits us out into a posh, high-tech entrance with inlaid marble floors, mirrored ceilings, and gigantic viewscreens adorning the walls. The doors are all polished steel. I try not to stare, but my heart is pounding again.

How long have they been operating here, in my neighborhood, without me even knowing?

I'm usually a pretty observant person. It's part of how I knew to get away from live acting at the first opportunity. You have to be a certain kind of tough to survive as a woman on stage or screen, and I'm not like that.

Of course, at fifteen, all I knew was that I was unhappy, but I knew enough to listen to my instincts. I now do it regularly, and I'm almost never wrong.

But this place flew completely under my radar until the people here saved me from Marvin. *This boss of Jake's is so clever that it scares me a little.* But whoever they are, I owe them thanks, too.

The arena isn't very big; it seats five hundred people in plush accommodations. I sink into my seat cushion and look down the slope of the ring-shaped arena to the cage below.

Two chain-link tunnels lead from opposite sides to gates on either side of the ring. The cage itself is an enormous chain-link dome reinforced with heavy steel pillars. Despite the comfort of the seats, the whole place has a hard-edged, industrial look to it: lots of brushed steel and rivets, the announcer's box on a tall metal pillar like a conning tower.

In the wall above the regular seats, I can see a set of skyboxes, each suite large and fronted with two-way mirrors to protect the privacy of those inside. The largest one projects out over the others a bit; I can see a tall shadow standing at the glass, very still. "Who's up there?"

"That's the boss's box. Holy shit. I didn't realize he was coming tonight." Cynthia suddenly looks worried. "Dave's gonna catch hell after the match."

"The boss?" I peer at the glass, remembering the respect with which Jake spoke of him. *Could I maybe ask him for help with the whole Marvin situation?*

"Yeah, the big boss. Some kind of computer billionaire. This is one of his pet projects—a private, unlicensed league run by his rules. The stakes are incredibly high—millions of bucks get wagered on these matches."

I turn to her. "Hope the pay for the fighters is that high, too." The chain-link walls of the cage remind me that Jake is about to go risk his neck for these people's entertainment.

"Oh yeah, the guy takes good care of us. He's kind of a recluse, though. He and his entourage tend to travel in secret." She frowns up at the box. "Almost none of us have seen his face—except for Jake."

How much does he know about what's gone on tonight? Was it his hand on the button when someone buzzed me in just in time? Does he know that Marvin hacked his building's security system on the fly—once while under guard?

"How do you ... get a message to him?" I ask as I stare up at that figure. "He needs to know about Marvin." Marvin who is dangerous: a sociopathic, hateful manchild with destructive skills and no self-control.

"Through Jake. He's one of the only guys here who talks to the boss directly. Usually we get email or a text." She looks me up and down as I open my coat and take off my gloves finally. "You feeling any better?"

"Yeah." I glance around again, checking for Marvin in the small crowd. No sign of him. But that only makes me look around for security cameras instead.

I can't find any in the arena, and I don't know why. Maybe they're too well hidden, or maybe there's a good reason not to keep any footage of the fights. Whatever the reason, not seeing any aimed at me makes me feel better.

"So why do you want to know how to get in touch with the boss? I'm sure between Jake and Dave, he'll get the whole story." She tilts her head my direction, eyes intent on mine.

"I get that. I just ... I'm worried that your boss will take the problem as lightly as Dave did." I hope that their boss wasn't the one who programmed their security or the man was no match for Marvin, billionaire or not.

"I seriously doubt that. He takes security very seriously. We've had very few problems. He is spread a little thin, though ... nobody around here knows just how many businesses he actually owns." She nods to herself. "Yeah, tell Jake what you want to pass along. He'll handle it."

"Okay." The seats are almost full as I look around. Not a familiar face in sight—especially not Marvin's. The fight will definitely start soon; the crowd's excitement is palpable as the big clock on the wall ticks toward the hour.

And then Jake will win and clean himself up and then take me off alone ... and I don't know what will happen then. But for the first time in my life, I'm really tempted to sleep with someone I've just barely met. And that's dangerous, illogical, probably stupid ... and feels amazing.

If living well is the best revenge ... then I almost wish I could make Marvin watch me living well without him. But really, I wish that he would just disappear.

Picked up by the cops, shot by this place's security, hit by a bus, struck down by a heart attack while stroking off to his *loli waifus*. I don't care which. I just want him gone.

For now, though, I feel safe and excited and interested in my life again, and I owe it all to Jake.

"So, you really do anime voiceovers? For like, the English versions? Any characters I know?" Cynthia seems genuinely curious. I list off a few character names from a few shows, and she nods in recognition at a few. But then the elegantly dressed, muscular announcer rises out of the top of the podium via a hidden elevator, and the crowd starts applauding.

I drop the subject as the announcer speaks in a booming voice, welcoming us all and announcing that the match will be beginning in five minutes. "Final bets must now be entered, ladies and gentlemen. Please call in your transfers to escrow now."

I look around and see everyone pulling out their cell phones to do so. I keep mine in my pocket; I don't have money for things like betting on this scale. But it's interesting to watch this crowd of rich people, celebrities, performers, and what looks suspiciously like bikers and gang members all laying down a ton of money for or against my hero of the night.

"He really hasn't lost a match in ten years?" I say wonderingly as the last of the bets are placed and the lights dim.

"Not one. That's Jake for you. If there's one thing about him, it's that he's reliable."

And then the announcer calls his name, and the music

starts, and we all stand to applaud as Jake comes strutting in through his tunnel, grinning and waving.

I stare down at him, my eyes widening. I knew that fighters went into the ring nearly naked except for shorts and groin padding. But I didn't know until now just how powerfully built Jake really is under his clothes.

My eyes trace over every curve and cut of his magnificent body—all that gleaming tanned skin, his broad shoulders, and high, tight ass under the black satin shorts. My gaze tries to follow his rippling belly and belt of Adonis down toward his barely hidden groin. I watch his chest heave as he waves to his fans, and then turns to acknowledge the slimmer, gracefully striding opponent coming down the chain-link tunnel toward him.

All it would take to have him tonight is an invitation, I think to myself as my toes curl in my boots. Staring down at him as he moves to his starting point and the other man comes in to take his own, I can feel the growing temptation to give him a very, very clear one as soon as we're back together.

But do I dare?

CHAPTER 6

J ake

THE LANKY, dark-haired fighter across from me isn't one for banter. That's fine with me—he was polite and waved to the crowd when his name was announced, and that's good enough to keep their attention. But now it's go time, and Chanchai here isn't just silent—he's barely looking at me.

Focus, buddy. I don't want to Nerf myself so badly that we don't give them a good show. It's no fun if I just land one on you while you're an inch from pulling your phone out and checking your Tinder. Or whatever has him so distracted.

I'm a pretty patient man, but lately I've been less than content with my job. I make a pile of money, have a lot of sex, and enjoy the company of most of my coworkers. But even though I'm showing enthusiasm with every expression and gesture ... I'm already a little dissatisfied with this fight.

Most MMA fighters on the underground circuit here in the United States are boxers, kickboxers, or other kinds of competitive athletes who would go legit if given half a chance. They're used to fighting by a certain set of rules, like weight classes or forbidden rules. I've fought guys like that for over a decade, and I'm so used to their techniques that it's gotten too easy to counter them.

But many underground fighters come from a whole different tradition of ring fighting, with their own rules and standards, making them unpredictable to me—and more of a challenge. That's why I get stoked when a guy from a totally different part of the world signs on against me.

But this one's acting like he's even more bored than I am. And that kind of pisses me off. *Come on, man, give me something to work with here!*

Then again, I'm in a perfect position to do something about his inattentiveness—by giving him a warning shot. Nothing game ending, just enough to wake him up.

The bell rings and we're off, circling each other, looking for an opening. I feint a lunge at him; he backs off marginally, but his black eyes are fixed more on the crowd than on me. *They're just a bunch of rich assholes placing bets on which one of us bleeds first. I'm the one in punching range.*

Shit, maybe the guy's just jet-lagged, and I'm being pissy for nothing. *I came into the ring irritated over the whole Marvin mess. That's probably all this is.*

I don't feel like chasing him around all day, so I fire a jab at his face to test his reflexes. And suddenly, unexpectedly—the magnificent bastard comes to life.

It's like he's suddenly decided I'm worth the effort; he ducks the blow and immediately tries to lock up my arm. He's faster than I thought, and his grip's perfect. I lean into his movement and manage to get out of his grip before he can fully immobilize the limb, but my arm still hurts as I pull it free.

Now it's my turn to dance away, bobbing on the balls of my feet, wary of the next surprise this guy will unleash on me. I'm smiling again, and not just for show. *Finally.* Chanchai has a gleam in his eye now, just the tiniest hint of a smile on his lips. Whatever he was distracted by before—or pretending to be distracted by—it's been pushed out of his head. He's all in.

The crowd roars as we trade our first blows; we test each other, then start circling again. He explodes forward in a flurry of hard, sharp kicks, forcing me to dodge and get some distance. He doesn't seem to expect me to go on the defensive so easy; his eyebrow lifts slightly in surprise.

So far, I've come at him with classic boxing moves. Nothing fancy, nothing that shows skill or training beyond that. Maybe he thinks I'm a one-trick bruiser with no depth or breadth to my skills. But nobody gets a decade-long undefeated record by being that lazy.

It takes perfect timing. I let him burn energy driving me back against the chain link—then bounce off it hard as he's got his leg up and drive him off balance. He flips to his feet—right into my elbow.

I pull the blow at the last second. Not much, but enough that I know he's getting back up. He hits the mat again, eyes wide and stunned but still moving. When the count comes, he's up in three, shaking it off and eyeing me warily.

That's right, buddy. I'm not just a bruiser. Now give it your all and let's entertain these bloodthirsty fuckers.

I'm a strategist. So's my opponent. We're sizing each other up as we circle and the excited crowd yells suggestions. I block them out, focusing everything on him.

The man to make the first move has a disadvantage, unless

he's accurately predicting a telegraphed blow. Once he commits, the uncertainty of his opponent's next move collapses to a few clear choices. Options for courses of action disappear.

Meanwhile, every action teaches your opponent about your skills, your style, and your level of aggression. Right now, we're both aware that we underestimated each other, and we're both on the defensive. But I'm aware of something else, too: all those people out there expecting a good show.

If I let them get too bored, the boss and I will take losses of another kind.

Fine. This might hurt a little, but it's worth it.

I'm tough enough to take some hits. Just as long as he doesn't make me bleed. I'm winning this match, even if I have to ice a few bruises to make it look good.

So, I go on the offensive—but not recklessly. I just make it look that way.

I go high with kicks to the head and punches to the body. I go low into leg sweeps, pushing myself not to stay on the same level too long. He isn't expecting my speed; I'm too big and bulky looking.

But those kind of assumptions are just another weakness that I can exploit. And exploit it I do—returning fire with a volley twice as fast and complex as his own. I connect a few times. Nothing as good as that elbow—but then he counters, and I take some hits myself.

Back and forth we go. The next time I connect, he backs off, holding his side, but recovers fast. Wearing him down is going to cost me. But I don't want to unleash any match-ending moves too soon.

The crowd is roaring. That's the part I love the most—making these matrons and captains of industry and government bigwigs scream my name when they would have let me die on the streets as a kid. Now, I rake in piles of their money with every single win, and all it costs me is lots of sweat and a little pain.

My opponent's response to being backed up against the chain-link is a thing of beauty; he bounds off the cage and unleashes another kick that I barely manage to block with both forearms. It's hard enough that I stagger, my arms going numb for a few seconds. Even more yelling from outside the cage; I do my best to block it out and focus on getting a counterblow in before he regains his balance.

With my arms recovering, I switch styles, snap-kicking him hard instead. His head tips back precariously, nearly off-balancing him; I see a few red flecks fly from his lips but know it's not enough to satisfy the first-blood rules. Instead, I keep at him, throwing an elbow into his chest and then trying to kick his legs from under him.

He flips sideways to evade me, landing on his feet. We're both breathing hard now, sweating, feeling the faint throb of developing bruises. Cage matches go until a man falls or bleeds enough. No breathers. No quarter at all.

As I'm circling with him again, my mind goes unbidden to the confrontation earlier. That shitty excuse for a man, putting his hands on Josie like that. I know Cynthia has her in the audience somewhere, and that she's safe and well looked after.

But that still leaves the matter of her stalker, whom Dave let get away. He could be anywhere. In her house. In the damn audience itself.

I gotta tell the boss every single detail after this, so I don't risk Dave leaving something out to cover his butt—

I'm suddenly ducking a haymaker followed by a spinning kick as my opponent notices my distraction and tries to take advantage. *Shit!* I quickly correct my mistake, laser-focusing on finding his next opening.

The boss told me once to give the whole fight a good five

minutes or more to make sure that the crowd gets what they pay for. With an almost guaranteed win, my performance would become less captivating otherwise. *It's been just over three minutes.*

I grab him around the waist while he's recovering and suplex him over my head and into the mat. I hear him grunt. I let go at once, flipping to my feet over him and backing up for just a sec to check how he's recovering.

Still kicking. He's on his hands and knees, shaking his head; he's wide open for a rib kick, but I know that will end the fight too quickly. I obviously feint that direction for the crowd's sake, and he rolls aside before getting to his feet.

Every time I hit an opponent hard these days, I've always had to check afterward to make sure they're not headed for the hospital or worse. It's not just a matter of my strength. Crazy accidents and overdoses may be minimized in the ring now, but some things just ... stick with you like that.

Besides, giving a tiny breather to my opponent helps me stretch the match out that precious five minutes.

I back him off again with a lunge and a few jabs before driving a knee up into his midsection. He barely manages to bend with the blow in time; the wind gets knocked out of him, and I keep lashing out until he's nearly up against the chain link again.

From this angle, I notice the boss's box is lit up, and spy his tall, lean figure standing near the glass. He almost always shows up for my fights, and tonight is no exception. And as always when I see him, I remember what he said to me the night that Billy died.

I understand that you're worried about potentially killing an opponent in the ring again. However, this situation was a freak accident, not an indicator that you're too hard on your opponents. You're capable of great violence, yes, but you're also capable of restraining your strength. You must not lose trust in yourself.

I block a back-fist that feels like Chanchai's swung a baseball bat at me. This guy's *Muay Thai* makes mine look like a pale imitation—but aside from that, he doesn't seem to have much scope to his fighting traditions. The boss has had me trained as a generalist: I'm not a lifelong specialist in anything, but the men he brought to train me were from every part of the globe.

Muay Thai artists tend to put their weight on their back leg and attack with their other three limbs. They also take a high stance. The reason I was able to suplex him easily was because my wrestling training let me take advantage of that. But right now, the relative immobility of that weight-bearing back leg means that every time I keep him moving, he can't bring all his strength to bear in *Muay Thai's* deadly kicks.

Keep him moving. Make him work to land a blow. I switch to *karate*, using my footwork to prevent him from sweeping me or landing a kick. He's panting harder now, his energetic attacks slowly taking their toll. I'm tired, too, and aching where he's hit me, but at least I've got the rush of a good match going.

I take our next stare down as a chance to plan my potential next moves. We have a few clashes left before I can knock him down and move on with my night. I already want a shower after trading blows with him under all these hot lights. And after that ... I'll get to see Josie again.

My opponent leg-sweeps me and makes me jump for it— and comes around again with a side kick that I block but which knocks me off balance. Now I'm pissed.

I go down, flip into a handstand, and kick out at him, driving him backward again. But it's a *Muay Thai* move, so of course he knows how to get out of the way before the blow lands.

I actually like that he's making me work for it. The boss usually makes sure to arrange good matches, but this one's extraordinary. Chanchai's sprung a few moves on me that I haven't seen before except on video.

I just wish we had a language in common, so I could ask if he wants to train together while he's in town. I'm sure this guy will just keep challenging me in new ways. I'm actually having fun for once.

I still catch myself wondering how Josie and Cynthia are doing. I was sure they would get along, and they seemed to when they left together. But I don't know what Josie's going to think of me after the fight. Or if she's going to be down with the things I'd love to do with her.

A quick view of the bottom of my opponent's foot forces me to duck just in time to keep my nose from being smashed. *Got distracted again.* What is with me tonight?

Except I know. It's pretty little Josie and the crisis that drove her into my life. It's the big-eyed, almost worshipful way she looks at me. It's the prospect of spending the night with her.

Gotta get through this guy first, I remind myself, a little annoyed. And so, on his next kick, I grab his leg and lock it up, then use it to flip him face first onto the mat.

This time, he stays down to the count of five, and comes up with just a rim of blood around one nostril. Still not quite enough. But I've clearly got him worried—and worried means aggressive.

And aggressive means mistakes. And thirty seconds later, he makes a big one.

He goes completely on the offensive; I dodge, redirect, sometimes block his blows, letting him pound away at me and wear himself down further. Only a few of his strikes actually land, leaving my forearms, thighs, and one cheek aching. I give back as good as I get, while the crowd goes insane on the other side of the chain link.

Five minutes. Time to clock out and go visit a pretty lady. Sorry, buddy.

Chanchai's anger and frustration doesn't lessen his skill, but his aggression leaves holes in his guard. I wait for my opportunity as he struggles to get a solid hit in. Then he leaves himself open for a split second—and I palm-strike him neatly under his jaw.

The startled look on Chanchai's face vanishes as his head snaps back, and he topples backward to the mat. I know he's out cold even before the counting starts. I stare hard at his chest and see it rise and fall normally. He'll have a sore jaw and bruises, but he's fine.

Then the referee reaches ten and announces me the winner, and I throw my arms up in victory as the crowd roars.

"Let's give it up for Jake Ares, our undefeated champion!"

I look around the crowd, and catch sight of Josie standing with the others, staring at me with wide eyes. Cynthia is cheering next to her, but all I can focus on is her.

CHAPTER 7

Jake

I'M HUMMING with adrenaline and endorphins from the fight and can't actually feel how much it's taxed me until I get back to my dressing room and take my first few swallows of sports drink. Normally, I don't even like the stuff, which tastes like weak fruity spit to me. But when I need what's in it, it tastes amazing, and I can't get enough.

As soon as the fluids and electrolytes start hitting my system, I'm suddenly swallowing the stuff down greedily. *Oh yeah. That guy made me work for it.* I take a second bottle into my bathroom with me and gulp it down, too, before stepping into the shower.

Once the hot water hits and my muscles relax, my body goes through its usual post-fight changes. I become aware of slight pain: my forearms ache, my muscles burn, every spot where Chanchai tagged me, or I bounced off the floor or chain link throbs dully with developing bruises. My knuckles and the tops of my feet are feeling it a little, too, but the heel of my hand is fine.

The jaw strike's part of my *Krav Maga* training. There's a spot on the underside of the chin that, if you hit it just right, will drop a guy with a minimum of force. The heel of the hand doesn't get easily injured from blunt force either, so it's win-win. He may not even bruise.

I started my career hitting hard, and a guy died. Now I hit smart, and guys go down, but I do my best to make sure they'll be walking away and able to go back to training. If I kill again, it will be deliberate, because I had no choice—and it will happen well outside the ring.

As I scrub down and the adrenaline ebbs away, I'm left with the endorphins and hormones rushing through me. My skin tingles like I'm high, and my dick stands up rigidly, rock-hard and hypersensitive. It's making it tough to bend down and scrub my toes.

"Crap. All right. Fine." I squirt some moisturizer onto my palm and take my cock in hand so I can finish up and actually fit into a clean pair of pants. *Not like this will take very long.* I usually pride myself on holding out, but my first nut after a fight is always hopelessly fast anyway.

All the more reason to get it over with before Josie shows up. If she's into me, I want to last long enough to show her a good time. If she's not into me, the awkward boner is going to be a problem.

I try to think about the groupie from this afternoon: the good fuck with a bad personality who took my cock like a champ. She wanted it "rough," so I didn't have to hold back as much as usual. My ass stings a little as the spray hits it: nail marks from her fancy manicure.

But when I close my eyes and think of her, trying to

remember her body against mine and her throaty voice moaning in my ear, the dissatisfaction I felt after our encounter rises up to haunt me. That nameless woman who wanted me to be her fucktoy in Mallorca. As if I could be bought.

I try to conjure up other encounters with other women ... but it's all variations on the same thing. They wanted my celebrity and my dick in their lives, but they didn't give a damn about me. *And they certainly never looked at me the way that sweet girl does.*

My fevered thoughts slide toward Josie again. That look she gave me after I saved her. The same look she gave me through the chain link of the arena. That almost worshipful surprise.

I want to see it on her face again as she trembles under me. I want her to cling to me, and whimper with pleasure, and beg for more. And as I let myself imagine that, my climax finally hits, and I groan through my teeth before sagging against the wall with relief.

Very temporary relief. My skin is still tingling, and I'm still thinking almost obsessively about sex. *Sex with Josie. Who thinks I'm her goddamn hero.*

I'm tossing my clothes in the hamper for the maid, a spa towel knotted around my hips, when I hear my phone ring with the boss's ringtone. *Shit.* I hurry out of the bathroom and pick it up immediately. "Hey, boss, sorry to keep you waiting."

"Excellent performance tonight," comes the calm, cultured voice with its Baltimore accent. "I notice that you're still pulling your blows."

"Yes, sir." I keep calm. I'm not the one who fucked up tonight, and I know I'm not in trouble. *But I'd better check.* "Is that a problem?"

"Not particularly. You kept it creative and didn't let him take advantage of your concern for his safety." I hear the soft chime of his cordial glass being set down; he always has it with him, sipping very slowly on any one of his rainbow of liqueur flavors. The guy's got the most elegant sweet tooth that I've ever seen.

"Okay, just checking. So how can I help you tonight?" I'm pretty sure I know what it is. *Dave, you poor dumb bastard.*

"The young lady who you rescued earlier. Is she safe?" There's even a touch of urgency to his normally calm voice.

It blindsides me. I know the boss has honor, and I know he's got a heart somewhere in that stuffy exterior, but I didn't expect him to be chivalrous.

"She's fine, boss. Cynthia's bringing her down to join me soon. I was going to put her up at the hotel. Any issue with that?" *Does he know Josie somehow?*

The weirdest thing about the boss is that as reclusive and private as he is, he seems to know everything about everyone. Some of the guys think he's psychic. Others credit his mysterious second in command, a completely anonymous hacker named Prometheus.

Me, I just think he's smart as hell and has all the right connections to get him the information he needs. He also has more intuition than any guy I have ever met—most women, too. I wouldn't play poker against him, that's for certain.

"I'm opening up the second penthouse for you. Get her address. I'll send a security team to investigate. This man must be retrieved." He sounds ... annoyed. That's a new one from him, too. He's normally as cool and serene as a stone Buddha in a rainstorm.

"Great. I'll pick up the key at the desk then. Do you want to talk to her directly? I don't mind relaying information, but she wanted to make sure you got all the information about this Marvin guy."

I can hear footsteps coming toward my door, and glance over my shoulder at it. I'm still in my towel. *Oh well. Guess the ladies get a bit of a show.*

"That won't be necessary at this point. She's likely very tired. Just her address and the make and model of her car. Those are the most likely sites where he'll be."

"She said she lives across the street from the back entrance. I'm assuming one of the lofts." Someone taps on the door and I call, "Be right there!"

"The loft complex. And the car?" I can hear the rapid rattle of computer keys over the phone.

"She didn't say, but I'm assuming it's the smallest, cutest thing in the lot." *Just like her.*

"Hmmm." More typing. "I'm seeing a pink Volkswagen beetle in the lot on that block. There's what appears to be a cartoon of a red panda in a dress on the door."

"That's definitely the one." *Why am I smiling so much? I don't even know if she wants me yet.*

But I'm plenty hopeful.

The boss coughs softly and I hear a beep. "Thank you for your assistance. I can run her plates and get the rest of her information from there. If Marvin is stalking her via this information, we can now anticipate his movements.

"Have a good evening. Take the next three days to look after the girl. Don't leave her side. I'll be wiring you a bonus as well as a stipend for expenses."

That's another surprise. "Thank you, sir. Is there anything else?"

"Yes. I'm calling Prometheus in on this one. You may receive texts. Answer them promptly unless attending to our guest's needs." More typing. "Do you have any questions?"

"Just one. What's going to happen to Dave?" Maybe it's Train Wreck Syndrome. Maybe it's just so I can tell Cynthia and Josie when they ask.

"I will be looking for a new night security manager." No

elaboration. His voice has gone back to almost toneless. "If you wish to apply for the position, let me know in the morning."

He ends the call, the sound of his typing cutting off mid-click.

He's even more eager to find this asshole Marvin than I am. I wonder if it's because he cracked the building security. That shocks me, just like the bonus and his offer. I'm not sure, but it feels like the boss is taking this all personally.

As for Dave ... I've got a feeling we won't be seeing him again. I don't like what that might imply, but I'm not going to say a damn thing about it.

I set my phone down and walk over to open my door and let the ladies in. "Hey. Sorry to keep you waiting."

Both of them give me the once over, and Josie starts blushing again, her eyes going big. Cynthia just grins.

"Hey there. I need to go meet my man for breakfast before he catches his flight, so I'm gonna leave you guys to it. Good night!"

I smile mischievously down at Josie, who swallows and looks me up and down again. "Sorry. The boss called while I was coming out of the shower. Come on in ... you can wait in the main room while I change."

She hesitates, doe-eyed and shy, and then nods and steps in next to me.

INTERMISSION

Carolyn

My cell phone wakes me out of a dead sleep. I grab for it blindly and flip it open. I realize it's Daniels yelling excitedly at me before I manage a belated, "Hello?"

"Moss! Get your ass up and get moving, you lucky bitch! We just had a giant break in your case!" He's almost manically excited. "You need to get the goddamn collar before the local PD grabs your guy. I'm having one of our techs email you all the info."

"Wait, what?" *Are you sending me after futile cases deliberately or trying to make a name for yourself through me—or both somehow?* I used to think his reasons for sending me after these five men all centered on revenge for me not sleeping with him. But both Prometheus and his own mixed actions say it's more complicated.

Maybe Daniels has an impulse control problem. It sure as hell seems like it right now. I stifle a yawn and the urge to say something sarcastic.

"We have an address for the illegal arena where this guy

fights! The cops are going to raid it at six this morning. I need you to get there first and get inside!"

I sit up, adrenaline racing through me. *Oh shit!* "Okay, sir, I'll check my email and be on my way."

"Do that. Don't screw this up." He hangs up, and the first thing in my head is *Prometheus*.

I get on my laptop and open the email from the field office, then open a secure chat box with Prometheus.

Are you back online?

"Please be there. I'm totally without backup." I skim the email and its attachments. Someone sent an anonymous data drop to the Detroit field office, who forwarded it to Daniels, thanks to my phone calls. They're not offering to mediate with police; too short-handed.

It's a lot of information. Not only the files on Jake Ares that I already have, but several photos of the supposed inside of the facility that the sender is claiming houses the arena. No photos of the arena itself, though.

A tiny alarm bell goes off in the back of my head and my eyes narrow. *Someone made a claim that the arena is at this address, but they're not presenting any direct evidence of it? Something stinks.*

There's also a brief security camera video of Ares punching an unidentified man in the face. I focus in on that—and just then, I get my reply from Prometheus.

I am here. Are you all right?

I smile with relief, a trickle of warmth running through me.

I'm fine, but I'm on the move. Someone has released a large amount of information about Jake Ares to the FBI and local police, and Detroit PD is planning a raid at six. I need to get inside before then. Can you help?

My response is a long pause. Then, unexpectedly, my phone rings again.

When I pick up, a deep, cultured voice with a light Maryland accent gently says, "Carolyn?"

"My breath catches and my eyes widen. "Prometheus?" I whisper.

"Yes," he purrs in response, that beautiful voice caressing my ears. I can feel it down to my toes. *What's happening to me?* "It was time that we spoke directly."

"What is it that prompted this?" My heart's beating so fast that I almost don't hear his answer. "I'm sorry?"

"I said that this 'break in the case' is a complete waste of your time and will lead to embarrassment if followed." He sounds gently regretful. "I apologize for being the bearer of bad news."

Is Prometheus involved in this somehow? I didn't even send him any of the information yet! "So, you already knew about this situation."

"Yes." I hear the clink of crystal and a sipping sound. "It crossed my desk soon after it was sent to the local police department. I have Detroit very well covered."

It sends a chill down my back. *He's here. He's in Detroit. I'm sure of it.* And the extent of his information-gathering abilities is far greater than I realized.

I find myself wondering just how dangerous he would be if he didn't have ethics. "What about the footage of Ares beating a guy up?"

"The claims are fabricated, and the video recontextualized. It's security footage of Mr. Ares defending a young woman from the man he is striking. It's a fragment of a much larger video, which I will supply to you." So calm. His voice soothes me some, but I'm still troubled.

"But the assault did happen at that address." That reminds me of something; I open the file on Ares and start looking for his employment information.

"Yes, as he is employed as security by a nightclub on the

second floor. The man in the video had been stalking his lover, and she ran to him for protection."

Moments later, I confirm it: the address released to the cops by the anonymous tipster is the address of the Iron Pit nightclub. Which Jake Ares has a completely above-board job at. *But who is the other guy on the tape?*

"Don't bother going to the address. The police will find nothing of consequence there and will soon be pursuing the man responsible for the false report." His voice is surprisingly kind. "Carolyn, trust me. Do not interrupt your sleep further."

"Is this the other hacker's doing? This YokaiPrince?" I still can't believe that I'm actually talking to the mysterious Prometheus after almost a month of contact.

"Marvin Ackerman, legally changed from Marvin Ecklund, age thirty-eight, a serial violent predator turned hacker who is currently stalking Mr. Ares's lover. I will send you the details. I assure you that his capture will do far more for public safety than that of Jacob Ares."

I consider all of this, still not quite buying it. "Why does he want to implicate that address?"

"Because he was forcibly ejected from the property, and because Mr. Ares intervened when he attacked Ares's lover." Keys click in the background.

"Oh, I see. So, this is a revenge thing on Ackerman's part." *Petty bastard.*

"Yes, and I'm afraid that the police department is going to suffer some humiliation as a result. You will save time, effort, and face by staying home. But I will make certain that you are able to collar Mr. Ackerman for causing all this trouble."

I stop short of asking if I'm just doing his dirty work in getting rid of a troublesome rival. He's never steered me wrong before. "Fine," I say finally. "Send me what you've got, and we'll make a deal."

CHAPTER 8

Josie

JAKE JUST ANSWERED the door wearing nothing but a towel. Left behind by a mischievously chuckling Cynthia, I hesitate inside with him; he shuts the door and locks it and turns to me with a smile.

It takes all my willpower to look up at his face. Not at his powerful chest, still gleaming and fragrant from his shower. Not his beautifully inked and sculpted arms.

I manage to speak after a moment. "That was awesome. Thank you for inviting me," I almost squeak.

He smiles softly. "I wanted you to see what I do when I'm not rescuing adorable young ladies from smelly assholes." He's making no attempt to move toward the bathroom as I walk toward the couch; instead, he follows me, close enough behind that I can feel the warmth rolling off of him.

"It was amazing. Are you okay after that?" My gaze snags on one of his forearms. Bruising is starting to show even under those tattoos.

He just grins and shrugs as he goes to the mini fridge in the corner and pulls out a sports drink. "Another occupational hazard. How are you feeling?"

"My face is just a little sore," I admit. "I barely noticed it during the fight."

"That's good. Well, so we're both a little sore, and I don't like how we met, but—"

"I like how we met," I interrupt him, and he blinks, the corners of his eyes crinkling. "You saved me," I explain. "Nobody does that. They just walk on by while people are getting hurt."

He swallows and his chest heaves. "I think you're romanticizing it a little. But ... you know I'd do it all over again." That gleam is back in his eyes—except now, it's almost like a steady glow, like an ember fully fanned back to life. "And not just because I like you so much, either."

I glance down demurely, warm all over from both his promise and his omission. I feel like I'm about to float off the ground from bliss. But then I notice something that leaves me even more breathless.

I can see the clear outline of his cock under the terrycloth. It's swelling, hardening ... rising as he grows excited.

For me.

This amazing, hot, gentlemanly man wants me. And yet he's staying quiet about it, not touching me. *It really is just like Cynthia said.*

I look back up at his face. He's watching me quietly. "Jake?" I ask very softly.

"Yeah." His voice is a little hoarse.

"Do I turn you on?"

Even almost certain that I know the answer, it takes all my daring to ask the question aloud.

"Oh yeah." He takes a shivery breath and looks down at me sincerely. "Little lady ... you say the word, and I'm yours until you decide to let me go."

... *Oh.*

I press my thighs together, muffling a soft whimper behind my lips. But then I reach a trembling hand out ... and lightly stroke my fingertips down his warm, rippled belly.

He lets out a low, musical moan. I do it again, exploring his chest, and he stands there panting and shivering but letting me trace every inch of him from belt line up to his shoulders. My left hand joins my right in caressing him, while he holds himself still, panting softly and letting out astounding little sighs of pleasure.

"See what you did?" he murmurs as the bulge grows beneath his towel. I watch his cock rise under the terrycloth, my eyes widening; it looks enormous. "Oh, baby," he purrs. "You've got me hard as a rock."

"Just from touching you?" My fingertips slide down his arm to the back of his hand, and then up over his belly. He tosses his head slightly and murmurs a little, low "oh," eyes squinted with pleasure.

"You have no idea what you do to me." His deep voice has a breathless lilt to it now. "I can't remember being happier to find out a woman wants me."

My heart lifts and I hug him, feeling the push of his cock against his belly as he shudders and wraps his arms around me. "Nobody's wanted me who I actually like before. I..." I'm whispering against his chest, and he trembles, cupping the back of my head lightly as my lips move against his skin.

I move away from him just a little, so I can drop my purse and strip out of my coat, tossing it behind me. His arms tighten around me again, and his big, warm hands start sliding over my body through my pink cardigan and jeans. I lean up to kiss him, and his mouth covers mine hungrily.

The kiss sends tingling heat rocking through me. His low rumble of pleasure as our lips caress each other only makes my heart beat faster. Feverish, I lean up further, arms thrown around his neck, kissing him back with more enthusiasm than skill.

Not that he seems to mind.

I unbutton the cardigan and shrug out of it too, wanting to feel those gentle, powerful hands on more of me. All the pain, loneliness, and fear are melting away as his kisses steal my breath.

It feels like he's so turned on that he can barely help himself; he purrs and groans low in his throat as he kisses me and shivers under my hands. My own little cries and whimpers of delight mix with his; his cloth-covered cock throbs hard as he presses it into my belly. When he nudges me back toward the couch, I go gladly.

The kiss breaks, and he stares down at me, panting. "You gotta tell me if I'm gonna need condoms or not," he rumbles hoarsely.

I squash a surge of self-consciousness. *Be real with yourself, Josie. This is what you want. And when will the chance come again?*

"Yes," I whisper, looking up at him. "You'd ... better grab them."

His couch has no arms; he lays me across it and takes off my shoes and socks before moving up to kiss me again. His hand slides firmly up my thigh. "You're sure?" he asks, his fingertips leaving trails of warmth on my skin.

"Yes." I'm nervous enough to feel it still, even under the soft glow of pleasure and desire, but I push on. "I'm sure."

He brings the condoms but doesn't move to put one on. He

helps me strip out of my shirt instead and starts kissing my neck when I demurely cover the cups of my bra with my hands.

His lips work magic on my skin, leaving my head lolling dizzily as he kisses me over my pulse and then starts nibbling and licking. I whimper, hands leaving my breasts and sliding up over his back instead.

When I lie back, he looms over me, kissing and teasing me with his mouth, running his hands over my bare skin and helping me to bare more. When the bra comes off, he takes one of my breasts in hand, his big, hot palm covering it soothingly.

"Do you like that, baby?" he breathes as his thumb slides back and forth over my nipple. I squirm under him, suddenly feeling like I'm suffocating in my jeans. "Oh yeah, you do." He moves down my body, warm breath blowing over my collarbone. "I bet you'll like this even more."

Suddenly his hot mouth engulfs my other nipple; he suckles eagerly, and I cry out, writhing, bucking my hips, pleasure nerves almost overloaded. He catches me in his arms, pinning my thrashing form against him as he pulls firmly on my sensitive flesh.

"Ohh!" I gasp, pressing my breast against his face reflexively even as I wonder if I can keep taking it. It feels so intense that it leaves me scared that I'll start screaming. "That feels so good ..."

He shudders and grunts as my nails dig against the taut muscles of his back. My voice keeps rising and falling, gasps and sighs pouring out of me uncontrollably. My pussy starts to clench with each long pull; my hips lift against him reflexively.

His hand leaves my other breast and tugs my zipper down. I lift my hips again and he unbuttons my jeans and starts pulling them and my panties off me. He removes them inch by slow inch, and then starts following them down my body.

I moan with disappointment as he lets my breast go, only to shiver as he kisses his way down my belly. His tongue swirls over my skin, circling my navel before trailing down the slope toward my pussy.

Realizing what he's after makes me sit up, gasping from nerves; he catches both my hands and squeezes them gently as his lips caress their way lower. I lay back, trembling, and he rewards my obedience by kissing the top of my slit tenderly.

His tongue darts between my pussy lips and caresses my folds, swiping slowly up and down as I fight his powerful grip. I groan through my teeth, straining, all of it reflex: it feels too good.

He lets go of my hands, and I grab his shoulders as he starts to lap at my aching clit. A shower of pleasure sparks bursts through me with every stroke; I have to fight not to grab his head and shove it against me. "Oh, it's good," I croon as he darts his tongue against me faster.

He has to hold me down. I've never felt anything as good as his tongue flicking firmly against my clit; my muscles start to clench and shudder with every swipe. His powerful arms hold my thighs apart and keep me from squirming away. There's no escaping.

"Yes ... yes ... *yes* ... oh don't stop, please ... I—"

He presses his lips to my lower ones and suckles lightly as he keeps flicking his tongue. The sensation drags a wail of pleasure out of me. My nails are digging into his shoulders, and I can't stop them. I can't stop any of this ... and I don't want to.

The sensation mounts with every flick of his tongue now. I'm trembling, tingling, ready to explode. My voice has broken into incoherent pleas.

Then he suckles harder—and I detonate, hard waves of pleasure rocking through me while I scream and roll my head from side to side and shimmy my hips against his face. My eyes are open but can't see anything. All I can do is feel, feel, and feel as my first orgasm rips through me.

I collapse, shivering and misted with sweat, as he raises his head. His hair is wild, his eyes wild, his cheeks gleaming. He wipes his mouth on the back of his hand and then reaches for a condom. "I've gotta have you."

"Do it," I gasp out, too limp and exhausted to move.

He tears off the towel, revealing his gleaming, thick erection, which trembles slightly with his heartbeat as he rolls the condom on. He grips my hips and lifts them as he kneels at the edge of the couch then his cock presses its way into me slowly.

"Ohhhhh," he groans. "Oh, baby, I wanted to fuck you so bad." He shifts his hips and sinks deeper, sending fresh shocks of pleasure through me. "Oh yes..."

I wrap my arms around him, holding him as he shudders and grunts his way through fucking me. It doesn't hurt. Instead, fresh ripples of pleasure run through me as he moves faster and faster.

He's completely into it, just as I was just before I came: his eyes screwed closed, his mouth open, gasps and shouts of pleasure bursting from him when our hips meet. I watch his face, fascinated, amazed by how just lifting my hips makes him shiver blissfully.

Our bellies smack together as he pounds away, faster and faster, shuddering shouts bouncing off the dressing room ceiling as he rides toward the same ecstasy. I'm panting and trembling again. As he gets rough enough to make my joints creak, my excitement peaks again, and I squeal and thrash under him.

"Aaah!" He buries his cock in me all the way, and I feel it shudder; his eyes roll closed and he jerks his hips wildly. "Yeah! Yeah ... oh ..." He sags over me, panting and trembling. "Oh," he breathes in my ear as I hold him. "Oh, Josie, baby. Oh."

I stare at the ceiling, stunned and triumphant. *I came. Twice, even. Oh God.*

"Stay with me tonight," I whisper in his ear as he settles over me. "In the hotel. Make love to me again."

He raises his head and smiles drowsily. "Gladly."

When we reach the penthouse, with its wall of windows, deep couches, and powerful central heat, he's on me again by the time we get our coats off. He kisses and nuzzles and nibbles and strips me as he nudges me toward the bedroom, leaving a trail of clothes behind. By the time he carries me into the bedroom and lays me on the bed, neither one of us has a stitch on.

I roll the condom on for him this time while he trembles and groans encouragement. By the time he joins me in bed and takes me in his arms, I'm wet and impatient.

He fucks me slowly, softly, purring words of pleasure and tenderness in my ear as his finger works against my clit. "I want you so much, baby. Let's stay here all weekend. Just fuck and eat and sleep."

"Oh, yes," I moan, as much from his swirling finger as from the suggestion. Then my muscles start to clench around him, tighter and tighter, and we both abandon words.

I lose track of time and climaxes as we grind and slide against each other; he goes through two more condoms, making sure I'm satisfied before letting himself climax. I drift, eyes half closed, and hold him as he shouts his ecstasy.

This second round ends with him stumbling back to me from the bathroom and dragging the blanket up over us as he lays down.

"I could really get used to this, baby," he murmurs against my ear, and my heart lifts despite my exhaustion.

I wrap my arms back around him and kiss his parted lips. "So could I."

When I sleep, there are no nightmares of Marvin, no sense of fear. I'm safe in Jake's arms, just like I wanted to be.

The Last Bout

I wake up half-rested, with no idea what time it is or how long I slept. Jake's spooning me from behind, slow breaths stirring my hair—and his cock brushing teasingly against my ass. *Oh. Hello there.*

My lover. This is my lover. I have one now, and we've been together all night and into the morning.

I roll over carefully and look over the muscled mound of Jake's shoulder at the wall-sized penthouse window. It's broad daylight outside; the snow has melted off some of the rooftops already.

I've been in bed with him all morning, having sex and sleeping. It makes me feel ... decadent. And that makes me feel daring.

Jake lets out a sigh and rolls on his back, his erection tenting the comforter. I giggle, giddy and excited as I reach under the cloth and run my fingers over his cock. He gasps softly as I explore the silky skin with my fingertips, growing more aroused as he does.

I like to make him moan. I like to make him shake. He can kick anybody's ass, but look what I can do to him with just my fingers.

The thought turns me on so much, I decide to do more than touch. I've already lost track of how many times we've made love ... but I'm up for more.

I'm sleepy, muzzy, and feverish with lust as I slide my body up over his. Jake smiles in his sleep and his erection throbs against my belly. I move up further, rubbing my pussy against his shaft, and he rewards me with one of those low, musical moans.

I take his cock in hand and run my fingers over it again as he shivers and moans louder. Memories of his deep, beautiful voice rising and falling with pleasure, each animal grunt, gasp, and groan from first kiss to climax, rush through my half-awake mind, leaving me hungry to hear them again.

I take hold of him and tuck the head of his cock inside of me, then start working my way slowly down its length. At once, he arches his back, hands flying to my hips, pushing his cock eagerly into me. His blissful groan makes my toes curl almost as much as being filled again.

Then he opens his eyes, face full of shocked delight, and I smile down at him. "Good afternoon, lover."

CHAPTER 9

Jake

I WAKE up slowly to the delicious sensation of my morning wood being softly embraced by a woman's flesh. Josie's scent surrounds me as the weight of her body sinks down over me and rises again, slow, embracing my cock fully with each downstroke.

It feels so good that I think I'm dreaming for a few thrusts, before the pleasure's intensity shakes me awake, and I realize that she's real and here—and riding me.

"Oh, baby," I purr drowsily, reaching up to run my hands over her hips. She smiles down at me mutely, hands braced on my chest, strong little legs wrapped around my hips as she pulls herself onto me. I smile broadly and lean up to kiss her as we move together.

She's already turned on as I start caressing her; her nipples are tight and her skin shivers under my fingertips. It's easy to get her panting and rocking harder against me. Then I slide two fingertips up against her clit and her eyes roll closed. Her hips grind on me deliciously.

Fucking a woman has never felt this good. Not just because of the tenderness of it or how she's gone from timid to bold in one night. But because right now, the physical pleasure is so intense, I couldn't stop fucking her if I wanted to.

I can feel all her soft folds, slick and hot, sliding over my dick as I sink home. I can feel every tremor and slight contraction. I ...

Oh my God, she's decided to fuck me raw. "Oh!" I gasp, and pant rapidly as I fight not to blow my load right then and there. "Oh, baby, you feel so fucking good ..."

She rides me a little faster, still smiling down at me like an angel, and I grind my head back against the pillow and can't do anything but make animal noises. Her small, delicate form has to fight a little to take me all in, but she's determined ... and I'm enthralled.

Every time she sits up on her knees and draws most of me out of her, my cock aches so hard for her embrace that I shake.

"Don't stop. Yeah. Just like that." I rock my hips as slowly as I can manage, my belly tight as I struggle for self-restraint.

I don't know how I manage to keep my fingers moving on her clit as she draws near climax and grinds on me faster and harder. Every roll of her hips caresses my cock in new ways. I thrust up to meet her, cursing and groaning and calling her my angel, swearing I'm hers, and meaning every word.

Then her eyes squint closed, and she sobs with pleasure as her pussy contracts around me. Her writhing drives me wilder and wilder until finally I rock my hips upward, yelling hoarsely. I nearly black out from the intensity as I climax.

Yes. Oh ... yes.

I empty myself deep inside of her, trembling and panting,

her name in my heart but nothing coming out of my mouth but noise. At the end, I collapse to the bed under her and contentedly drift, eyes closed, barely conscious.

I open my eyes while she's still catching her breath. She's curled on my chest, already starting to fall asleep, as I lie there completely relaxed under her. I stroke a hand down her back, and she shivers with delight.

I'm tingling from my belly to my knees; my dick is still buried inside of her, but like the rest of me, it's now completely relaxed. Her breasts slide against my chest as she breathes, but even that can't turn me on right now.

I've never blown that hard in my life.

I smile and lean up to bury my nose in her tangled hair. I've got no idea why she decided to fuck me without a condom, but slight risk or not, I can't possibly complain. I've never even fucked anyone without a rubber before and ... this was definitely one to remember.

I guess she's on the pill. Weird, she said she doesn't date. Maybe she takes it for health stuff or was just being proactive.

I don't know. I'll ask her about it later. But right now ... I'm just waiting until my dick recovers, so we can do it all again.

Unfortunately, I don't get the chance. I've tucked her into bed and gotten up to shower off the sweat when the boss's special ringtone goes off for the first time in over a day. I grab it out of my coat and retreat to the bathroom to answer.

"Have you turned on the news recently?" comes the question instead of a hello. I'm instantly on high alert. At my confused silence, he goes on: "I'll assume no, then. There was an attempted police raid on the arena this morning."

I almost drop the phone in shock; it's enough to drive thoughts of more sex right out of my head. "What? Holy shit—what happened? Are we blown?"

"Not at all. We had advance warning from an asset of mine.

The concrete bulkheads concealing the sub-basement levels were lowered and the elevator control plates switched out to exclude access. To outsiders, there was no remaining evidence that the sub-basements even exist."

My jaw drops. *That is some James Bond shit right there.* But then again, this is the boss; maybe I should expect it.

"The hacker responsible for the security breach was unable to determine the exact location of the arena within the building due to the lack of CCTV in those areas. The police raided the licensed nightclub upstairs and found nothing."

I feel my blood pressure rising as I listen. *Fucking Marvin. It has to be.*

"So, they scared off a bunch of clubgoers and embarrassed themselves." I rub my face. *Fucking Marvin swatted the arena, because he couldn't find either of us.* "Are we suing?"

"Legal action will take place after Marvin Ackerman has been located and either collected or silenced. He can do no further damage to us online thanks to Prometheus, but thanks to your former coworker, he had a full hour to penetrate the building's systems and gather information."

I don't have to ask if he's talking about Dave. I already know. "Okay. So, what do you need from me?"

"The police will continue looking for you and for the young lady with you as will this stalker. We must find Ackerman before they do. But the only lead we have on his current location is his obsession with Josephine Cotter."

His voice is very serious and my heart sinks. "Josie really can't deal with facing him again. I can protect her, but—"

"I have no intention of allowing him anywhere near the young lady. Right now, my goal is to assist the FBI in collaring him. But it will require the young lady's cooperation. I want you to persuade her. I will give you two hours to do so and contact you again." He's so calm that I wouldn't know it was a crisis if he wasn't giving me details.

"Hold up, hold up. You're working with the FBI?" As far as I knew, the boss loathes law enforcement.

"No, I have an asset within the FBI, and I am working with her. I wish for you to meet with her and plan some means to draw Ackerman out." There's a slight edge to his voice. "This isn't optional, Jacob."

I stiffen slightly. In the other room, I can hear Josie stirring and making soft sounds. "Of course not. I'm just surprised you're handing the guy over to the authorities."

"Your new lover has a legitimate career to safeguard. If she works with the authorities against a documented stalker in an above-board way, both she and my asset will benefit. And so will we."

He's still almost serene. *How does he do it? Meditation? Xanax? Or just good acting skills?*

I'm a little worried about the completeness of his information. "How did you know that Josie's my—" I start.

He cuts in a bit sharply. "Two hours ago, Ackerman attempted to blackmail her with an audio recording of your lovemaking. Prometheus intercepted the messages, destroyed the originating computer's operating system, and is monitoring for the release of any further copies of the recording."

I feel my knuckles crack from my fist clenching so hard. Rage runs through me, lava hot, making my muscles thrum. "Go on."

"We theorize that he took over the microphone on her smartphone and used it to spy on her. We do not know how much he was able to pick up from your interactions with her or Cynthia. But as she is a voice actress with a distinctive voice—the audio recording may ruin her career."

As I think of sweet Josie's croons and sobs as I gave her her first orgasms, my rage only intensifies. That pile of trash Marvin just tried to turn some of the best moments of my life into blackmail material. *He probably jerked off to it, too.*

"Boss," I say in the calmest voice I can manage. "Let me kill him. Forget the FBI agent—"

"No."

His voice has gone from serene to implacable in an instant. I catch my breath, the single syllable like a splash of cold water on my face. "Sir?"

His tone gentles a shade. "Follow my instructions, Jacob. Not simply because if you do so, things will work out better for all of us, but because you are not a killer. You never have been. Leave that work for those of us who will not be sickened by such things."

"Sir, I've killed two people—"

"No." Now he sounds a bit annoyed. "You accidentally killed *one* person. The other was killed by an overdose thanks to an irresponsible trainer. And you still torment yourself over both." He sighs. "I fully understand the desire to beat this foul little man into a paste, but he must serve as an example to his kind and face very public consequences. Only once he fades from the spotlight can he be eliminated gracefully ... and you will not be the one to do it."

I struggle to control my anger and finally win, giving over with a huff of breath. "Yes, sir." *Damn it. He's right.*

"Just focus on the girl's safety ... and on persuading her to talk. I'll give you Special Agent Moss's phone number. Make certain that you arrange a meet within the next two hours. We are on a very short timetable."

"I'll get it done." He hangs up, and I stare at my phone before setting it down.

Fuck.

The urge to beat Marvin until he never gets up again still

burns in my muscles. I take a cold shower to cool it and slap myself awake. I have a hard talk with Josie ahead.

I don't think I can tell her about the recording. I don't want her to have to deal with that kind of humiliation. But I'm sure as hell warning her to mute her microphone when she isn't on a call.

And when I run into Marvin again, I may not kill him—but he and I are going to have one hell of a showdown.

CHAPTER 10

Josie

I'VE BEEN in Heaven for almost a day, and the crash back to Earth hurts.

Jake's doing his best to soften the blow. He's got both his hands folded around mine, cradling them while he gently tells me the facts. But each one hits me hard ... and I get the feeling that he's holding back some of what he knows.

"The boss wants you to shut off your phone completely when not in use or at least mute the microphone and cover the cameras. There's evidence that Marvin was tracking you using your phone."

Numb, I nod and reach into my jacket pocket—then sigh with relief. The battery's dead—it's probably been dead for hours. I keep it turned off as I charge it. "It's been off for a while now. Don't know how long. I didn't check it."

He doesn't look too relieved. "Well, that was how he was tracking you. Do you have any idea where this bastard is living?"

"No, he um ... he got thrown out by his mom after I told her what he was doing to me. He's got money, though. But no connections to anyone that I know of." It makes me sick to think about it.

Every time Marvin faces consequences for harassing me, he comes back twice as hard. It's like he plans to force me to love him and thinks that will somehow actually work.

But Jake won't let that happen, and neither will I. "Okay, got it about the phone. But what's this about an FBI agent? That was a lot to take in."

"Her name's Carolyn Moss. The boss called her an 'asset,' so I'm guessing she works with him a lot. We have to work together to find a way to draw Marvin out so she can make the collar. He's got a lot more than just stalking and attacking you to answer for, apparently." He can't make eye contact suddenly.

What did Marvin do? "Like what?"

"Well, I don't know much, but it's enough to make him interesting to the FBI, especially after he tried to use both the cops and the feds to raid the arena. That was pretty much the dumbest thing he could have done, given that the cops are already looking for him," he says. "So ... yeah. Your stalker is gonna go away for a very long time if we can just draw him out." He rubs his big palm over the back of my hand, and my belly tightens with desire despite the stress.

Can't we just climb back into bed to make love again and forget about all of this?

But his serious expression already tells me otherwise. I brace myself and nod, tears in my eyes. "There's a lot more you're not telling me, isn't there? Stuff I missed while I was ... asleep."

The sweetest, deepest sleep of my life—absolutely peaceful. And before and after, sex and tenderness, and falling deeper in love every minute that I spent in his arms. I want that back ... but Marvin is trying to ruin it all for good.

Jake gives me a worried look. "Baby, there's really no need to get into all the ugly details. They'll just make your stomach hurt."

I stare at him sadly, wanting to just let him shield me from whatever it is, but... "Jake, I need to build a case against him—"

"You don't have to worry about that anymore. It's bigger than what he's done to you. Everything you've documented will be entered into evidence in the larger case." It sounds like he's repeating something he was told. I'm not sure why that bothers me, but it does.

"Jake ... I know it's not just about me. But please let me know what you're protecting me from."

He glances over at my charging phone. "So far, he tried to expose the arena, he released the security tapes edited so that they only show me hitting him and not what he did to you, and he..." His voice catches in his chest, and he has to force out what he says next. "The boss's hacker Prometheus intercepted an attempt to blackmail you."

What? "How?"

"He threatened to release embarrassing information on you to try to ruin your career if you don't come out of hiding and agree to meet with him." He's being vague; his eyes are avoiding mine again.

"What embarrassing information?" I cast back through my memory to anything scandalous that I have ever done and come up with exactly nothing. "Did he make something up?"

"I don't know. I honestly haven't gotten a copy. But whatever it is, it's nothing you could possibly have to be ashamed about." He squeezes my hand tenderly. "That asshole is doing shit to throw you off balance, scare you, and try and force you into the open. But we're gonna work with this FBI agent to turn things around on him."

It doesn't actually sound like I have a choice—and that bothers me. But that's not Jake's fault. "So, what's the plan to do that?"

"I'm not sure." He frowns, sitting back against the headboard. I crawl onto his lap and curl up, and he wraps his arms around me snugly. "But I do know this. If we want him to make a mistake, we have to stir him up. Get him angry."

"That part makes sense." An idea starts forming in my head. *What would drive Marvin crazy enough to make him come out in public?*

"All my life, I was taught not to provoke guys. I was supposed to make peace, be nice, and never make anybody angry. Jake ... this won't be natural for me. But he deserves it." He deserves every misery and humiliation that he's ever inflicted on others. And then some.

"You'll find something to set the bastard off. I'll keep him from coming near you, and then the FBI lady will grab him. We can move on without him." He nuzzles my hair gently.

"I hope you're right." I tuck my head under his chin. I'm scared of what this disruption is going to do to what's been growing between us. But Marvin's determination to fuck up my life is not going to make me give up on Jake.

I won't let him. I decide who I'm with. Not that piece of heartless trash.

"Okay," I say finally, doing my best to be brave. "Let's arrange a meeting with this woman and figure out how to draw Marvin out of hiding."

I'm in the shower a few minutes later when it hits me that not knowing what Marvin was trying to blackmail me with still bothers me. As nice as it is to have Jake and some benevolent computer security guy running interference with me, I still feel unprepared because I don't know.

When I get out and dressed, my phone is charged. I turn it on apprehensively. I can feel Jake's eyes on my back as I stand there listening to the message alerts chime again and again.

340 missed phone calls in the span of ten hours. That number right there tells me more than I ever wanted to know about Marvin's obsessiveness. Missed text messages: 634. Emails: 216. They're not even filtered to where I can read them; I locked down my phone at Jake's request on the way to the hotel.

Marvin, what is wrong with you? He probably spent those ten hours red-faced and spluttering, drool on his lips, and his skin covered in sweat from rage even in the cold. Calling and calling and texting and sending the same email over and over.

I wonder if his mother ever lived in fear of him like I did before meeting Jake. Has she been working her way up to throwing him out for years and only used his stalking me as an excuse?

"Make him lose his temper," I stare numbly down at my phone. "It looks like he's already there, Jake."

"Yeah, well, when we get done with him, he won't have his pride or any friends left either. And soon after that, he'll lose his freedom and all access to a computer." He rubs my shoulders soothingly.

I stare down at my phone full of crazy and think back on the last few days. "I'm worried about this."

He sighs into my hair. "I don't like it, either, baby, but at least we'll have help."

We. He's gotten attached, too. That's a light in the darkness to me right now. If we can just get through this together and have something solid and real at the end, I can endure all this garbage.

And even if the "we" part doesn't work, the other point is that I have help now. I'm not facing Marvin alone.

I try to take comfort in it as Jake makes his phone calls to arrange for the meeting with this Special Agent Moss. I actually feel a little better that it's a female agent. The men around me have been kind, but I'm willing to bet none of them have actually been stalked or harassed themselves.

The sad thing is, I can pretty much bet that any woman in law enforcement has dealt with some creep's attention. Just like any woman with a touch of fame, a woman with any authority becomes a target for the kind of men who can't stand that they have it. Men like Marvin.

Telling my story to a stranger who knows the territory is going to be easier than telling it to someone who doesn't. I learned that the hard way when I started reporting Marvin's harassment.

"He just sounds like a fan to me. Have you considered talking to him? Oh. you have. Have you had your manager talk to him? Oh. Well, maybe it will blow over, and he'll get interested in somebody else.

"This has been going on for two months? You documented all of it? Well why did you wait so long to do anything? Oh, you did. You have a list of things you tried? Interesting.

"I'm still not sure you have a case here. The guy's just got a crush on you."

The detective that Detroit PD assigned to me was a young, blond man who stared at me like I had grown another head when I explained to him that I wanted a restraining order and wanted to document Marvin's harassment with police. He simply could not understand, no matter how much I explained, why this was a big enough concern to involve the police.

He was also astonished when I went over his head to ask for another detective. His superior, a middle-aged woman, rolled her eyes when I explained my reasons and did not reassign me, but gave him a talking-to behind closed doors while I waited. He came out red-faced, took my statement, and gave me no further trouble.

I shouldn't have had to spend so much time explaining something like this to a guy who has never felt that particular terror before, that the threat to me is real and that I'm deserving of help. But at least I know that Jake will never do that to me. He's already proven that more than once.

Jake finally hangs up. "We're meeting at your loft in an hour. The police and bureau have already been through with their evidence techs. You should be able to move back in tonight if you really want to. But meanwhile, you can pick some stuff up while you're there."

"That sounds good." My stomach flutters at the idea. "Let's get something to eat along the way." I'm not actually hungry. Just buying time, terrified of what I'll find when we reach my loft.

As it is, even with a stomach full of chicken and spinach omelet, I get pretty shaky once we finally drive up to the front of my building forty-five minutes later. Jake parks his truck on the street and helps me out into the thin, icy rain. He walks close behind me as I buzz us in.

My heart aches from beating so hard as we check my mailbox, which is stuffed full of handwritten notes. I leave them for the cops to look at and go upstairs. And there ... a huge surge of relief washes over me as I see that my steel apartment door is dented and scratched, but intact.

When I check inside, everything is where I left it. Nothing is broken, stolen, or moved. "He never got through the door." I sigh with relief as Jake hugs me from behind.

"Doesn't look like it." I turn around, and he plants a kiss on my forehead. "That's a relief anyway."

When I check through my big, mullioned side window at the

parking lot, though, I realize that my cute little VW bug is another story. A rectangle of police tape surrounds my parking space, which contains nothing but sprays of broken glass.

"Oh shit," I gasp, putting one hand on the cold pane in front of me, tears blurring my vision. "That creep busted up my car."

I love that car. It was a gift from a major animation company after I signed a ten-year deal to voice characters for their children's department. The first big gift of my entire performing career.

I cry at the window as Jake stands with an arm around me and then I turn and cuddle into his chest until my tears dry up. "That's probably what he was threatening me with. Bastard. But I still wouldn't have caved in to him."

I'm not sure, though. There might be more to it than that. If he was satisfied with smashing up my car, he wouldn't have tried to kick in my door. "Jake...?" I look up at him, bracing myself for more evasiveness.

"Yeah?" He kisses the end of my nose.

"I still want to know what all these messages were. I can't get it out of my head. You said your boss's hacker was tracking what Marvin did. Will he talk with me?" It comes out of my mouth with more determination than I thought I could muster. "I need you to at least try."

"Well, I'll do my part and ask him. After we talk to the agent, though. The boss wanted that handled fast." He hesitates, then asks slowly, "Are you sure you want to deliberately let Marvin terrorize you, though?"

"What do you mean?" *What do you know, Jake? What do you think you're protecting me from?*

"What I mean is, Marvin was threatening you with blackmail bad enough that it even freaked the boss out. I'm actually pretty glad I didn't get any real specifics, or I'd probably want to murder the guy." His eyes flash with such sincere anger on my behalf that my suspicions lose some strength.

"Jake ... don't talk like that. I just found you. I don't want to lose you to a prison sentence because of some prick." I brush the side of his face with my hand. "I'm just saying that I don't want to end up blindsided by something really ugly because someone hid the truth from me."

He winces and looks down. "I don't plan to let him get close enough to you to blindside you with anything. But ... it's nice to hear that you'd rather keep me than use me for your revenge."

"You're not someone I ever want to use," I murmur, and he kisses me so tenderly that now there are tears in my eyes for another reason.

He still hasn't really answered my question, though. "So, you think that just by hearing whatever he wanted to send me—his threats, his anger, whatever—would have scared me so badly that just listening to it would have served his purpose?"

"Half of it." He slides his hand up and down my back slowly, soothing me. "He wanted to scare you, that's for certain, and he wanted to break you down. So why listen if all it will do is hurt you?"

That finally makes sense, even if it doesn't get me the information I may need.

"Contact Prometheus if you can. I really don't need any nasty surprises." I consider. "Though I think I'll just ask him for a summary instead of actually listening to what Marvin said. I'm sure he was abusive as hell, thinking about it."

"Good." He sighs with deep relief and then kisses the side of my neck lingeringly.

I feel an ember of desire deep in my womb and press against him ... just as his phone rings. He backs off slightly with an apologetic grin. "I think that's the fed."

Crap. I move away while he answers, going to put the teapot on.

Special Agent Carolyn Moss is a tall, elegant woman with a long, almost-silver braid and a quiet, frank manner. "Let's get each other up to speed, first off," she says calmly as she walks in my door. "I'll go first."

Once we're settled around my dining room table with peppermint green tea in hand, she pulls a printout from her briefcase and slides it over to me. "Your stalker, Marvin Ackerman, is actually a suspect in a couple of data breaches as well as harassment, assault, and possibly distribution charges. He's been following the anime convention circuit across the country for ten years. He's been banned from several conventions due to his behavior and is in legal proceedings with two of them. Multiple female voice actors in the United States have restraining orders against him."

She peers at her notes with a scowl. "In addition, his mother has been hospitalized multiple times due to his assaults but has refused to press charges on him."

I turn cold inside. *You bastard. Your own mother?* "She really did dote on him because she was so scared of him."

"It certainly appears so." The agent looks between the two of us and lifts an eyebrow. "How much do you know about Marvin Ackerman?"

I go over the whole story while Jake holds my hand under the table. Now and again I sip tea and do my best to calm down. My stomach is in knots before I even get to the part about his chasing me across the street into Jake's building.

She nods. "This corroborates the reports you left with local police. When Ackerman's name came up in conjunction with the 'evidence' he anonymously released to us, we became aware of the connection between his 'senseless beating' and the stalking incidents."

"You ... know then that Jake was just defending me, right? He gave Marvin every chance to let me go." It's terribly important to me that Jake not take the fall for Marvin's bullshit. He's my hero. He deserves everything good—and none of this woman's nosiness.

"I did see that. The whole security tape was supplied to me, and I watched it start to finish. Jake saved you from assault, kidnapping, possibly worse. He's not subject to arrest for his intervention," she says. "However, now that he has come under scrutiny by both Detroit PD and the bureau, Ackerman has decided to take his case to the public. He released the edited version and his explanation of the events online and is trying to character assassinate both yourself and Jake."

Her solemn statement makes Jake tense up and makes me go cold inside. "We can't let him get away with it," I gasp, and then turn to Jake. "Can your friend Prometheus help remove—"

Jake's eyes widen slightly, and my cheeks start to burn. I have blurted out that name without checking with him to see if it's all right first. But it's the FBI agent's response that really unnerves me.

She goes completely rigid, eyes widening slightly. "You ... know about Prometheus's involvement is this? What do you know about him?"

I go silent, horrified, as she turns expectantly to Jake.

CHAPTER 11

Jake

W<small>ELL</small>, shit, honey. I can't even be mad at Josie right now; she's innocent, inexperienced in anything outside the law, and she's very upset. But her blurting out Prometheus's name like that suddenly has the FBI agent very interested in everything I know about him.

"The guy's a computer expert. He handles IT and internet security for my boss. Why?" *Just play it cool. If she thinks I don't know anything—which is very nearly true—she'll just move on.*

"Do you have any idea how I could get in touch with him directly? As in face to face?" Her stare unnerves me a little. She's as intent as an opponent in a match.

"Face to face? Uh ... look, Special Agent Moss, I hate to disappoint you, but I don't even know if the boss has ever met this person face to face. I don't even know if it's a man or a woman."

I'm an expert at looking cool under pressure, but my guts are suddenly rebelling against the steak and eggs I just ate.

The boss says she's an asset, I remind myself. *The boss must have the means to control her if she gets too nosy. But holy shit, going to him means admitting what Josie just let slip, and that I didn't think to warn her against it.*

Focus. Why is she suddenly so interested in the boss's tech guy?

"He's a man," the fed says suddenly, sounding so wistful that I really start to wonder what her interest is. "I'm just trying to reach him."

"If you really do know the boss, he'll have an easier time putting you in touch with this guy than I can. I literally only know him through texts and emails." From the disappointment on her face, I can tell two things: she really wants to find this guy, and so far, the boss hasn't helped her.

Which means I can't help her either. All I can do is apologize and hope she isn't the type to abuse her power for the sake of revenge.

She seems startled that I know of her connection to my employer. But it's the only real leverage I have over her, and she's starting to get nosy. I'm sure her bosses won't like the idea of her connection to a billionaire who runs an underground MMA league.

We lock eyes for a second, and then she nods slightly. "I guess I should have expected that. It's in line with what I already know." She frowns and goes quiet for several heart-freezing seconds. I wait things out with Josie squeezing my hand hard.

"Let's ... continue with the Ackerman case." She sounds resigned, and Josie's grip loosens as I feel myself relax a little. "I have created a psychological profile for Mr. Ackerman based on all the available data. Your experience falls in line with what I have been able to observe.

"Mr. Ackerman is a narcissist. He may have a variety of

other psychological ailments, including his propensity for violence, his misogyny and apparent pedophilia, and his stalking behavior. But all of these stem from his extremely over-inflated sense of himself, arrogance, disregard for others, and obsession with validation and support for his delusional beliefs about himself."

"You get those in the ring or the gym now and again," I comment. The gigantic tantrum that Marvin threw, not only in response to Josie's running from him but in response to my slugging him, wasn't the act of a man with a good grasp of his place in the world. I look over, and Josie is nodding, too.

"Please go on, Agent Moss." She sounds very thoughtful.

"Well, an individual like him thrives on a sense of control and importance. Unfortunately, Marvin is a social reject with a poor grasp of appropriate behavior and no interest in working to improve his situation. He has high intelligence and a highly specialized set of skills connected to his interests—largely in the area of computers.

"Because he is not receiving what he believes to be his due from those around him—or from who catch his interest from afar, as you did—he will first seek to force them to conform to his wishes. When that doesn't work, he will seek to punish the nonconformists for failing him." She takes a sip of her tea. "This is good. Arabian?"

"Russian." Josie is staring into her cup distractedly. "I'll give you a few bags. The company name's on them."

"Thank you." Agent Moss looks between us, and that wistful look comes back to her face. I wonder if her search for Prometheus might just be personal, and not a matter of her job at all.

But when she goes on, she's all business. "His rage and obsessiveness stem directly from this need for control, and his violence is merely the expression of that. He seeks absolute power over those he obsesses on, but he is not in control of himself."

"With a guy like that in the ring, you can set him off really easily," I muse. "Once a fighter loses their temper, they lose control, and they make mistakes."

"Yeah, we were talking about that earlier. It makes it really easy to provoke him." Josie presses her lips together and looks down at the tabletop. "He wants to destroy me because he can't have me."

"And, very likely, because you don't conform to his narcissistic fantasies. He's created a role for you in his life and views it as your obligation to step into it. The more that you assert that you are your own person and have no interest in obeying him, the more enraged he becomes." She glances at Josie's front door. "He very likely injured himself doing that, which forced his retreat. That would also explain why he has been committing no further physical crimes, nor attempting to find you physically."

I have absolutely no problem thinking of that putz, already with a split lip and missing tooth thanks to me, fracturing a bone or two venting his giant-toddler rage against that damn door. But Josie looks worried.

"We have to draw him out of hiding," she says, still staring distractedly into her tea.

"Yes, otherwise the locals will move on quickly given Detroit's high crime rate, and our help will dry up as fast as our other witnesses." Moss's voice reminds me a little bit of the boss's—it's almost stonily calm.

"That means we have to make him angry." Josie swallows. "I have to make him angry. Really angry."

"That shouldn't be difficult with his issues." I take a big swallow of tea and stifle the urge to protest. Anything that puts the crosshairs back on this sweet young lady, I am not for. But we're running out of time, and I don't know what this bastard will do next. "He's the one who committed a felony in full view of a bunch of security cameras."

Josie gets that thoughtful frown on her face again. "I think I know how to make him so angry that he comes out in the open."

"Oh?" The agent focuses on her solemnly as I have to put my hand over my mouth.

It's necessary. But it isn't safe, and I know that before she actually says what she's planning out loud.

"He's trying to defame the both of us," she says firmly. "So, I'll go to the court of public opinion, too. I'm going to hold a press conference and tell everyone the truth about Marvin Ackerman and what he's done to me."

My back teeth start hurting. *Shut up, Jake, let her be brave.*

"That's definitely going to be effective in both stemming rumors and exposing the suspect," Agent Moss agrees. "Chances are that if the conference is announced beforehand, he will be unable to resist showing up."

"And then we can grab him." I catch myself. "*You* can grab him."

Moss glances at me and nods. "Yes. But I should warn you that when someone like this suffers from a severe enough narcissistic injury, he becomes even more dangerous. He may disregard his own safety for the sake of what he sees as vindication."

Josie looks worried, then lifts her chin. "Jake will be there. You'll be there with a damn gun, and it will be in public. If it will end all of this, I'm willing to take my chances."

But I'm not, I want to say, even as the agent and I nod agreement.

CHAPTER 12

Josie

I'VE NEVER CALLED a press conference before. But after bringing the police and my lawyer as far up to speed as I can without mentioning Jake's boss or the arena, I go online and do just that. I sadly announce that I may be taking a break from my voice-acting duties due to the actions of a persistent stalker, and that at the conference, I will outline the details and what I plan to do.

I make the announcement on social media, my website, and on fan sites for my work. It takes a couple of hours. Jake's already called his boss, who insists that we hold the conference in the nightclub during the day when it will be closed, but he can fill the room with security. That makes me feel a bit better about all of this.

I'm surprised by the size of the response. Anime bloggers, people in the industry, and news reporters all start RSVPing and writing in with questions. I get dozens of them in the first hour, and they just keep coming in.

There's also hate—not much proportionally, but even though I haven't mentioned specifics yet, a couple of anons and a couple of non-anons start spewing at me. Interestingly, though, they're all angry that I'm thinking of retiring ... all but one, which encourages me to do so while calling me a whore.

I forward the hate messages to Jake, who sends them on to both the FBI agent and Prometheus to try and trace. I answer questions I'm sent but gently refuse all requests to release a transcript or details before the actual conference. The idea is to physically draw people out, and those details are the bait.

So am I.

"I don't feel the best about you putting yourself at risk like this," Jake admits late that night, after he's finally pulled me away from the computer with the dual temptations of sex and pizza. He cuddles me close as we catch our breath and wait on our delivery. "He could get his hands on a gun."

"Maybe. But there's going to be an armed FBI agent and your boss's security team there backing you up in protecting me." I hesitate, looking up at him worriedly. "Um. Dave's ... not going to be leading the security team, is he?"

He gives me a wry look. "Dave doesn't work for the boss anymore, baby. I'll be heading the security team myself."

"Oh." *Good.* I immediately feel guilty for thinking that. Dave's single act of buzzing me into the building *had* helped me. But everything after that was a train wreck thanks to him, including him letting Marvin escape. "I feel a lot safer with you in charge."

He smiles and nuzzles me and kisses my neck. I squash a surge of desire, not wanting to give room service a show when they finally come up. I've gotten bolder ... but not *that* bold.

Later, plans solidified, belly full, and body spent from all the sex, I curl against a sleeping Jake and think again how lucky I am to have found him. *It would drive Marvin crazy to realize that if it wasn't for him, I may not have run into Jake at all.*

I absolutely won't allow Marvin to drive us apart now. No matter what happens, no matter what he says or does, I'm staying right here.

I'm still a little scared, though. It keeps me awake long after Jake, even drowsing in his arms. I just wish I knew what Marvin's going to do.

The next evening at seven, the nightclub opens early—but the bouncers are only letting in anime fans and reporters. They've been told to make a note of anyone coming in who fits Marvin's description and let Jake know right away.

I've dressed in a simple lavender skirt suit with a lace blouse, hair in pony-buns, makeup girlish and conservative all at once. When I walk into the dim, quiet cavern of the club, the big flat screens lining the walls are showing clips with my anime characters. I'm on the low stage, a podium in front of me, a file of notes on top ... it's just like giving a talk at a regular convention.

I fall into my role of the innocent young voice actress as my eyes scan the crowd. No sign of Marvin yet.

I know that there are twenty guards scattered throughout the room—ten in street clothes, ten in the club's uniform of BDUs, ball caps, and tight T-shirts with the club's Iron Pit logo, all waiting to jump on Jake's word. Jake's right at the edge of the stage in a looser BDU shirt but the same basic uniform, checking in with his men on a fancy microphone like secret service guys wear. But I'm still very nervous.

Finally, seven thirty rolls around and the doors close. Jake is listening intently to something on his mic. I can see the guards starting to search the crowd. Marvin is here somewhere; the bouncer must have spotted him coming in.

Now we have to make him show himself in the crowd

enough for the others to pounce on him. Stomach fluttering with apprehension, I step up to the mic and turn it on.

"Hi, everybody," I say in the kindest, most cheerful voice I can manage. "Thanks for coming! I wanted to tell you all what's going on that has made me think of retiring and what I have decided to do about it. I'll then take any questions that you have. Okay?"

A ripple goes through the crowd. Usually, when I sweep them with my gaze like this, I'm trying to connect with them, to meet their eyes, to make them feel more recognized and included. But right now, I'm just looking for Marvin.

The image on the screen changes suddenly to the start of the security video of my beating. "A lot of you have sent me messages on the fan sites and my social media asking me about this videotape. I'm here to set the record straight.

"The first thing that you should know is that the video that was released online is only a small part of a much longer one taken by the security cameras upstairs. That segment was released online by a hacker who calls himself YokaiPrince. In reality, he is the man in this video. His name is Marvin Ackerman."

Another ripple goes through the crowd. I see a few heads nodding, a few sets of eyes rolling. He's known on the online forums, probably for being as terrible a person as he is offline.

"Ackerman released the tape segment and other misinformation online and even tried to get the police involved in order to try and get the other man, my boyfriend, arrested, and damage the reputation of the business where he works.

"He is lying. I am about to show you the entire video to prove it." I force determination into my voice, lifting my chin, and channeling the pluckiest of my characters even though I don't feel it.

I glance Jake's way. He's watching me like a hawk, gives me a smile and a thumbs-up. It galvanizes me, and I go on.

"Marvin Ackerman has been stalking me for the last six months. This is a matter of both public and legal record. I filed a restraining order against him early in the situation, and he has consistently ignored it." I hear gasps of shock and quiet curses.

My anger, which I have barely felt through all the fear, stokes up now as I let the anime world know just what kind of a man Marvin Ackerman is. It gives me even more strength.

"He has come to my work. He has stolen my private information. He has sent me thousands of obscene, threatening emails and texts. He has forced me to change my phone number three times."

Many in the crowds are starting to look angry and horrified, too. A reporter from Tokyo, an older, bearded man with glasses, is shaking his head and muttering disapprovingly in Japanese in the front row.

"Two nights ago, I was leaving my home to go on an errand when I discovered Ackerman leaning on my car." The crowd moves more as the guards continue to search. *Wish it wasn't so dark in here.*

Maybe I should have told them how he smells instead of how he looks. I look over at Jake, who is starting to look frustrated, too.

Keep going. He'll lose his temper and start yelling or rush me eventually. And then they'll grab him.

"He chased me away from my door, so I ran across the street toward this building, where my boyfriend Jake was supposed to be getting ready to start his shift. I banged on the door. The shift manager buzzed me in.

"Marvin hacked the security door and got inside while I was looking for a place to hide. The rest is on the tape. I'll narrate."

The footage starts, one camera angle on each of the four screens. I hear gasps and glance back to see myself banging on the glass door trying to get the attention of the man in the black pickup. The man who, thank God, turned out to be Jake.

There's a collective gasp as Marvin runs up behind me on the video and grabs me, slamming my face against the glass. I feel my stomach clench as my own image struggles and bleeds, remembering my terror.

Seconds later, Jake pulls open the door and comes to my rescue.

"As you can see, when my boyfriend hit this guy, it was because Ackerman had chased me down and was trying to beat me unconscious in front of him. Ackerman would not let me go after multiple warnings. You can see it for yourself."

I suddenly feel hollowed out, exhausted, as if I've vomited up some poison. Tears brim in my eyes. "If he's not found and made to stop, I don't think I can have any kind of public life anymore, not even voice acting."

I hear shouts of outrage start up, angry rumbling, and for a terrifying moment, I think they're angry at me somehow. But then I hear what they're saying.

The Japanese reporter calls Marvin a beastly idiot. A big bear of a guy, who only resembles Marvin in beard and profile, is grumbling about how his daughter's going to cry her eyes out if this bastard gets his way. A few women are in tears.

Holy crap. The realization that they're on my side shocks me pleasantly. I've been so depressed for so long that I never even thought of asking for help from the same people who made my career.

I bow my head over the podium. "Thank you so much for your understanding—"

"Ohh!"

A cry of rapture echoes over my microphone. Female. Familiar. It's my voice.

I freeze in shock, just as I hear myself sigh. "That feels so good ..."

Horrified, I switch off the Bluetooth microphone just as I hear Jake yelling for the sound guy to cut the feed. The noise stops as I look around in confusion.

"Hold on, everyone! Something's wrong with the sound system." I smile out at them, blushing furiously while waves of cold shock run through me.

What was that? What did Marvin do?

I turn to look at Jake—and when I see the absolute fury on his face, I know. And he knows I know.

The mic on my phone. The night Jake and I first made love. That monster spied on us! He recorded it! He's playing it now!

"I'm sorry for the inconvenience. I'm not sure what's going on—" I stammer, even as the full horror of this invasion of privacy drops on me like a million tons.

"Listen!" comes a screech from the back of the room. All heads turn—and suddenly the crowd jumps back from a single spot, as if repelled by something. I crane my neck and see Marvin charging out of the shadows, holding up his cell phone.

The sounds of my first lovemaking session with Jake spill from the phone's small speakers as he brandishes it. It can barely be heard above the shouts of shock and outrage erupting all around him. But his voice strains so hard to be the loudest that it cracks.

"Listen to your perfect princess whore herself out to a man she just met! She's a whore! She's a fucking whore! Here's the proof!"

My jaw drops in horror as he crows on, running up to the stage, so determined that he shrugs off a takedown attempt by one of the guards. "He's not her boyfriend! They're not in love! She just likes him because he's hotter than me!"

Beside me, I hear a feral growl of rage. I turn around and see

Jake coiled like he's about to leap off the stage and pummel Marvin into a red paste.

I have to stop that confrontation before it starts, or Jake will go to jail.

Screwing up my courage, I put my fists on my hips and raise my chin. "Well hell, Marvin!" I shout.

The crowd goes quiet, listening for my response. I lean over and stare him right in the eye in front of everyone as he struggles toward me. The sex noises are still coming from his phone. It takes all my strength to ignore them and go on.

"The back end of a hippopotamus is hotter than you, Marvin. It doesn't take much!"

He goes absolutely still, jaw dropping. I watch his face go from white to red to white again as laughter ripples through the crowd.

"And would you turn off your porn ringtone already? We get it. You're a pervert. It's obnoxious." I'm channeling thirteen-year-old mean girls, my voice dripping with disdain.

"But that's ... you!" He seems absolutely astounded that I'm not collapsing in tears and begging him to stop. "That's you on here!"

"No, it isn't!" My reply is snotty and dismissive. Inside, part of me is collapsing, my heart aching and burning in my chest, the public humiliation threatening to overwhelm me. But then, once again, the court of public opinion speaks.

"Man, that doesn't even sound like her!" the bearish dude grumbles. Heads nod. "And even if it was, what kind of sicko stalks a girl and records her sleeping with her boyfriend?"

"He's not her boyfriend!" Marvin screeches, even as the men converge on him through the pressing crowd. "I am! She's mine!"

"No, I'm not!" I shout back, with the venom and fury of months behind it. "I'll never be with you!"

I hear the crowd start screaming before the fog of rage clears enough for me to see what's freaking them out. I see something dark in Marvin's hands; he's pointing it at me, his face purple and twisted with hate.

Everyone went through a metal detector, I think in numb disbelief before I realize that the object is polymer. A flare gun.

The podium is too narrow to take cover behind.

Time slows. My eyes widen. I tense to throw myself to the side, flame blooms in the wide barrel, and Marvin grins crazily with tears in his eyes. Then something big slams into me and carries me to the ground.

It's Jake—covering me, shielding me. I hear Marvin scream in frustration and then the heavy thud of security personnel plowing into him. And for a few happy seconds, I think that everything's all right after all.

We got him! He tried his best and failed again and again, and now the FBI will take him out of our lives forever!

"We did it, Jake!" I gasp, turning in his grip to hug him. He's strangely unresponsive.

Someone is yelling for an ambulance.

"... Jake?"

He's limp in my arms. And that's when I smell it. Scorched fabric ... and burned flesh.

"Jake!" I cry in horror, sitting up. I catch sight of the mess the flare made of his side ... and collapse over him, my vision going gray and then fading entirely.

CHAPTER 13

Jake

I WAKE up staring at a hospital wall. I'm propped up on one side and the other is bandaged from my underarm to the top of my hip. My head's fuzzy with drugs, but I can still feel the scraping pain under the bandages.

I look around, taking in the small suite, the slightly wilted bouquets on the shelf across from my bed, and the tubes and sensors stuck to or into me. I can't roll over to look behind me, but I hear a rustling sound that tells me there's another bed in the room.

Then I smell a familiar perfume and realize who its occupant is. My heart leaps. "Josie?"

"Jake?" I hear the thump of bare feet on the tile floor, and then she's hurrying around to look at me.

It's definitely not the same night, I realize as my heart sinks.

She's not in that cute candy-colored suit anymore, but in a pale pink flannel nightgown with kittens on it. "Hi, baby." I give her a smile despite my confusion.

"You're awake!" Her face lights up and she leans over to gently hug me, avoiding the bandaged area. "I missed you so much. How are you feeling?"

"Like I took a flare to the ribs for love, baby. How do you think I feel?" I see her face and quickly reach over to squeeze her hand. "It's fine. You're worth it."

Her eyes brim over with tears, and she smiles. "Thank you, Jake. For everything."

"No problem. So, what did I miss? How long has it been?" I lean up for a kiss ... but her smile fades slightly before she gives me one.

"Three weeks," she admits finally. "You were sedated. They had to do skin grafts and stuff. But it's healing up and everything."

Three weeks? Holy shit. That's a lot of missed fights and workouts. But that's fine. I've come back from broken limbs and concussions.

Burns heal, too. And I'll wear this particular scar with pride.

"Okay, sorry, that's just kind of crazy to me. What happened after I got shot?" I'm trying to keep my voice cheerful, but mostly, what I feel beyond the shock is ... relief.

It's done. I defended my new lover, whose face I want to wake up to every day, and whose name I'll never forget. And despite taking a serious hit ... I survived it.

"Marvin went to jail for attempted murder on top of everything else. Agent Moss brought him in, and we haven't heard from him since. The trial starts next week. I'm testifying against him." She sounds steady, resolved. It's great to hear.

"I will, too, if I can drag myself out of this bed by then." I really hope so. Right now, my body, normally so capable, feels heavy and useless.

"Well, the docs say you're healing up well, though you'll have to deal with wound care and maybe some plastic surgery." She looks sad, almost ashamed.

"Hey, now, none of that face, honey. I'm gonna be fine. I'd block a real bullet for you if I had to." *I mean it with everything I have.*

She nods, swallowing hard and wiping her eyes. "Sorry. It's just been a long time, and I've been so worried. The police released a formal apology to your boss about mistaking his place for another, illegal business with the same name and conducting the raid. And, um, I've still got all my fans, and nobody actually believes I'm... you know... a whore." She chews her lip and looks away.

"I'm so sorry that he did that, baby." I reach up clumsily to brush my hand through her hair.

"Did you know he had recorded us?" she asks in a tiny voice.

I freeze, then close my eyes. "Yeah. I did. But I didn't know what to do about it."

She frowns. "I told you I didn't want to be blindsided."

"And fucking Prometheus told me that all copies of that damn recording were gone." *She never should have known that he had tried to weaponize those wonderful memories against us.*

"Except for the personal one that Marvin kept on his phone," she corrects, pain on her face. "I ... still have nightmares about that moment."

"I'm so sorry, baby. Is this ... a deal breaker?" I'm not used to feeling unsure of myself anymore. Not since I became a man. Even with all the sedatives, I feel a cold surge of worry run through me.

But then she laughs and shakes her head, and the feeling dissipates instantly. *Oh, thank God.*

"I'm not happy that you did that. But I know you meant well. And then you nearly died trying to protect me. That's even what you were doing when you hid the truth from me, however much I hate that you did it." She caresses the back of my hand with her small one.

"I won't do it again," I promise, and she gives me an almost stern look.

"Well, you'd better not, because I can't be with someone who does it habitually." Her tone is firm, and I nod, then grunt, wondering why even moving my head hurts. "Besides, from now on, you won't be disappointing just me when you do that."

"Sorry?" She's brushing her hand against her slim belly. "Did I miss something?"

"I'm pregnant," she admits.

I stare. *Oh ... shit.*

"You ... um ... know that time that I decided to wake you up —" she starts, and I cut her off.

"Honey, that was in my top twenty best goddamn memories. Of course, I remember it." The pleasure. So strong, so sweet, so full of connectedness. An orgasm so intense that my memory couldn't hold the sensation of it clearly.

But then I realize, and my jaw drops.

Holy shit. She didn't raw me on purpose. "Did you forget the condom?"

She nods, blushing furiously. "I'm sorry. I just ... you see, I can't really get too mad at you for screwing up big because ... I did, too."

I let my head drop to the pillow, puffing out my cheeks in surprise. "Well damn."

"I want to keep it," she says tentatively. "But I, um, wanted to talk to you about it before making a decision."

I stare at the wall, blinking slowly, then look back at her. "I ..." She tenses, and I feel a rush of warmth inside of me as I see my chance to actually wake up to her every morning ... just like I already want.

"The kid's gonna need a daddy," I say firmly. "And I need you. So, I guess that's that." I don't know if I'm ready to be a dad —or a husband.

But I'm used to rolling with the punches and coming out on top.

"You sure?" she breathes, bouncing just slightly, like she can't contain herself.

I crack a grin despite the pain. "Yeah."

Josie smiles.

THE END

EPILOGUE

Carolyn

"So, you're telling me that the Iron Pit really is just a damn nightclub, and Ares is just a bouncer? The whole damn thing about an outlaw boxing ring in the Detroit warehouse district is just hacker rumor-mongering?" Daniels huffs and splutters over the phone, as openly disappointed as a kid.

"That's what the police said in their report. The whole thing was just a hacker on a revenge spree taking advantage of internet rumors to try and 'punish' the nightclub staff and Josephine Cotter." Except there's so much more than that.

I'm absolutely sure that the arena exists, though it may not exist in that building or even within Detroit city limits. But compared to Marvin Ackerman, Jake Ares is barely a criminal. And he's certainly not a danger to others.

Watching him take a goddamn flare gun shot in the side to protect the woman he loves has done something to me that I didn't expect. Nobody has ever cared for me enough to take a risk like that. And so now, trying to wrap things up in Detroit, I've found myself wrestling with a lot of loneliness.

Daniels throws something against the wall of his office with a grunt and a thud. "Fuck! I can't believe this!"

"Hey. I saved the bureau some embarrassment and grabbed the guy who caused all the trouble for you." I use a mollifying tone, secretly smirking.

He huffs out all his air. "Yeah, okay, that part's true. So, you've finished up with the cops and that club owner?"

"Everything's done here. Took a bit because of all the legal issues, but yeah, everything's finally sewn up." And I'm glad. I spent all of February in Detroit and am now completely sick of it.

He doesn't know that while I was wrestling with Detroit PD bigwigs over custody of the suspect, trying in vain to get a face to face with the club owner and securing witnesses, I was also spending every night searching the city for Prometheus.

I begged him to meet with me. He wouldn't do it. I cried over it, swore over it, and followed every lead I could find ... to end up absolutely nowhere.

Finally, I managed to settle myself down, give up, and work on forcing myself to get over my loneliness instead. Because I'm not looking for him for the sake of work.

I'm looking for him because for the first time in my life, I find myself missing someone who I have never met.

"Well," Daniels says finally. "Guess you're on to your fifth subject then. Good luck catching this one. Nobody's ever even seen his face."

"I'll manage, sir."

"Fine. I'll secure you a flight out to Baltimore tomorrow morning. Be ready to go by seven." The connection breaks.

I go pour myself a brandy from the hotel wet bar before trying Prometheus again.

"Carolyn?" It startles me; the phone barely rang. "You're not asking to meet again, I hope. I've made it clear that I am a very private man."

"Yeah, you have. I didn't call for that. I just ..." *Wanted to hear your voice again.* "I'm wrapping up here and headed to Baltimore."

"I see." A pause. I hear a clink of a glass and a sip. "I assume you'll be calling about your next case once you get there?"

I blush. I've become dependent on him, and he knows it. "No, this call ... isn't about work either."

"Oh? Then what?" His voice is very gentle. Like he's already guessed. Or maybe is happily anticipating my answer?

Wishful thinking from a lady with a stupid crush.

"I just wondered if you would like to talk. You know, like normal people." *Like a man and a woman.*

"Intriguing." He sets down his glass with another clink. "Please go on."

And suddenly I can't stop smiling.

THE END.

SIGN UP TO RECEIVE FREE BOOKS

Sign Up to Receive Free E-Books and Audiobook Codes.

Would you like to read **Savage Hearts** and **other romance books** for **free?**

You can sign up to receive free e-books and audiobooks by typing this link into your browser:

https://ivywondersauthor.com/ivy-wonders-author

©Copyright 2020 by Ivy Wonder All rights Reserved
In no way is it legal to reproduce, duplicate, or transmit any part of this document in either electronic means or in printed format. Recording of this publication is strictly prohibited and any storage of this document is not allowed unless with written permission from the publisher. All rights are reserved.

Respective authors own all copyrights not held by the publisher.

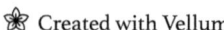 Created with Vellum

www.ingramcontent.com/pod-product-compliance
Lightning Source LLC
LaVergne TN
LVHW011718060526
838200LV00051B/2949